THE POOL
ARRIVAL

Brent Knowles

PUBLISHED BY:
YourOtherMind Media

The Pool: Arrival

ISBN 978-0-9938499-2-3

www.brentknowles.com Visit Brent's
Writing & Game Design Site

Discover other titles by Brent Knowles at:
www.amazon.com/author/brentknowles

CONTENTS

CHAPTER 1

Goodbye, Earth

My love, remember those assignments, first day of school, where you tell your class what happened over summer vacation? Not looking forward to that next fall. What will I possibly have to say? My fate is to suffer several boring weeks stranded on an empty planet with only two dull sisters and one control-freak of a mother. Nothing interesting will happen. Nothing at all.

Not the way I wanted to start my final year of high school!

And I will miss you. My phone won't even work, mother says, we won't be able to talk at all. Anyways, I'm late, and I should go and I don't want to, not at all.

All my love!

See you soon!

I send the message to Salva before I change my mind. If he thinks me silly, so be it. No time for regrets. I'm late and my grandmother's urn is awkward to carry. I don't know why the crazy lady bequeathed her *remains* to me but I'm sure as sun stuck with them.

I tuck the urn under my arm and rush for the elevator but Viv's voice erupts from my phone, startling me.

"The shuttle's waiting, Miranda!"

Her face appears on the small screen, glaring at me. Her coffee-colored skin is darker than mine, though not as dark as mother's. I wouldn't ever admit it but I'm rather envious of Viv's skin. Would die for it, as girls my age two hundred years ago might have said.

"On my way, Big Sister." I stick my tongue out at her, but she's already disconnected the call, doesn't see me.

I'm halfway to our private elevator and out of habit I pause, checking the newsfeed painting itself on our wall. My luggage squawks at me, the train of suitcases jostling to a rattling stop behind me as I view the weather forecast. Mother surely paid to ensure we'll have a clear launch, but you never know, right?

Twenty eight degrees Celsius and not a cloud in the sky. As usual.

In the screen's reflection I double check my appearance. My bangs have fallen over my forehead again and I set the urn full of grandmother's ashes down to tidy my hair. I'm sure my sisters will tease me but I know I'm going to look like a cavewoman by the end of this summer. We are roughing it on an unforgiving planet.

2

Might as well be pretty while I can.

I still don't understand why grandmother chose this year to die (really, could she have been more selfish?) She should have waited till after my graduation, next year. Her death makes no sense but none of us will ever know why she did it; she was *offline* when it happened.

I give my skirt a solid tug and then lead my clumsy luggage into the elevator. The ride down is smooth and the view spectacular, but I've seen the cityscape a thousand times before and focus instead on my phone, scrolling through all the goodbyes and bestoflucks and hugskissesandtears.

Most of my peers use icons to differentiate themselves online because we all tend to look alike nowadays, with our dark skin and darker hair. The past two generations have seen an increase in *indulgences*, our parents paying plenty to have our genetics modified, satisfying the latest fads. The icons are essential, else there'd be chaos online.

My friend Mae is a pink rabbit carrying a shotgun, Jann-jann a female tree-hopper 'cause she likes that kind of thing. Me... I'm myself and not just because my skin is lighter than most (for some reason the genetic tinkering our wiggly embryos undergo failed to make me as dark skinned as I should be) but because of our family. We are the grandchildren of Grandmother Terrasta, the daughters of Drea Terrasta. We are the elite of the Distinguished. Makes us a big deal. High expectations and all that.

Where others blend into the anonymity of our huge world, my siblings and I must be mindful of how we present ourselves. I exit the elevator and try to smile; the buzzers flying overhead are not just recording video of me, they also monitor heart rate, perspiration, and brain activity. Am I scared or excited to be launching into space for the first time? Am I going to miss my friends? My shopping? These will be the topics of the gossip sites all weekend.

Let's be honest — I do appreciate the attention. But I hate how the newsfeeds rattle on about how many siblings I have, as if implying that mother is overly promiscuous, that it is inappropriate for a gal like me to have a brother and *three* sisters. Personally, I think they are jealous because more often than not mom refuses their requests for interviews and vidshoots. They once offered her a reality show but she said no and I know that made Adira and Viv kinda proud of her. Me: not so much. I'd have liked to be on a proper show. Would've been fun.

See, I'm not smart like my little sister Adira, who is always reading, even books, which is kinda weird nowadays. I'd rather watch videos and listen to music. And I'm definitely not as driven as Viv who will eventually run the family business, will become the most important woman in all the world, like mother is now.

I enjoy parties and clothes and having fun. Doing all that on camera, regular-like, yeah, I'd have loved it.

But now I'm on the street and the transit center is right in front of me, made especially for this occasion. A gleaming steel shuttle rocket is cradled by the launch scaffolding, all of it in the shadow of our family's apartment tower.

I take a deep breath. I am abandoning everything I know and love but it will only be one summer. Big deal, right? Grandmother once lived on that planet of hers for half a year.

'Course I'm not grandmother and I can't be. Women like her are not made anymore (literally). My phone squawks and Viv's face reappears (not that I can't see her across the street, in realtime). I wave to both versions of her.

Mother and Adira have their heads together, talking about something I'm sure I (and ninety-nine percent of the world) have no real interest in. The rest of my family stands behind them, conversing with various orange-suited technicians, an entire herd of the commoners milling around.

I resist the urge to cringe.

"Ta da, here I am," I say as I study the street. My bravado is a cover. I'm hoping against hope that *he* will be here. I never asked him to come, 'course, but I hinted and now I'm hoping. Everybody who matters is here, a parade of the rich and powerful. I admire the ruffled gowns worn by mother's generation and the longer dresses gals closer in age to me, wear. Far to the back of the crowd are the lesser notables, including SanFran's mayor and the governor, sweating uncomfortably as if the *just right* sun is too hot for them. Probably irritated that they weren't important enough to warrant a handshake with mother. (But there's no sign of Salva Durand.)

A person born a few hundred years ago might have recognized a street such as this, with its skyscrapers and grid-ruled street, but that's not because we haven't advanced since then. Nowadays any neighborhood in any (respectable) city chooses how it looks. The key to life on Earth is choice. Anything can be changed.

"You're late," Viv barks. She's a rather attractive woman but when she's scowling… she's kinda frightening.

I snap my fingers and my luggage starts across the street. I'm pleased with myself for having corralled them (and myself) on time. And really, shouldn't everybody be?

But then I stop.

I've forgotten the ashes. Grandmother's ashes. In the hallway.

BRB I text and then turn the phone off. I've been shouted at by Viv enough in my life. I leave my luggage to find their own way and rush back to our suites.

Grandmother is the entire reason for our ill-timed voyage. Can't leave her behind.

Never expected to find them all dead.

There's robots everywhere. Sweepers and dusters; moppers and those tiny robots that crawl around the kitchen counters sucking up spills. I'm used to them rattling around, not lying motionless.

They deactivated themselves the moment our apartment was deemed *unoccupied*. I've never been anywhere this quiet before. Once we are on that other planet, is it going to be like this? All the time?

I tiptoe past the robot corpses towards where I left grandmother's urn. Except it isn't there anymore. I look up and down the hall but I'm sure I placed the urn right under the vidscreen. Maybe I'm wrong, maybe I forgot it in the great room.

I walk past a hallway full of closed doors, expecting some robot, gone mad from loneliness, lunging (yeah, I know, it's only been a few minutes, but really, who knows what goes through a robot's mind, right?)

My bedroom door is open and I remember closing it. I almost send the signal to activate security but stop myself; no way will I endure Viv and Adira's teasing all summer. Instead I confront my doorway.

All my stuff is still there. The video posters are playing (with volume muted). Much of my wall space is devoted to the Squishsocks, the *fave* band of the trendy upper class this month.

My dressers and closets are closed up all snug and the door to my bath is shut, as are the stairs down into my private virtualization chamber (a.k.a. school). Everything is in its place. Except that grandmother's urn is in the middle of my room and Salva Durand holds it.

Now, I'm a practical young woman. My heart almost never flutters, my knees almost never weaken. No matter how handsome or pretty the object of my attraction I'm unflappable (as is proper for any guy or gal in my pharmaceutically moderated generation). Yet if a man is going to *swoon me*, it should be Salva Durand. Calling him tall or handsome is a disservice; he's muscled, his suit rippling in the right places as he hands the urn to me, our fingers brushing. He's paler than most of our generation but on him, the lighter tone, works.

"Mr. Durand?"

"I took the liberty of using your window, Miranda," he says, grinning, his use of my given name sending a delicious shudder through me. Only with family or intimates is such familiarity acceptable, but I'm wondering more about his entrance than his etiquette.

The window never should have opened for him. If I were any other gal, I'd have accepted it. After all Salva is Salva. But I'm Miranda Terrasta and even a Durand can't override my safeties. I almost complain but then he wraps his arms around me. He's never been this affectionate before and I'm taken aback, trying to pull away.

His grip is unbreakable.

"You tease me, Mr. Durand," I say.

Given my place in society it is simple enough to research any guy or gal I'm attracted to. In seconds I'm able to track bloodlines, determining how their genetic profiles have been influenced over the generations; I have access to school records and medical histories and delinquency reports. I'm even capable of analyzing social chatter (what past lovers say about how my prospective indulgences treat their partners). More than any other young woman at any other time in the universe I'm equipped to make educated decisions about who climbs into my bed.

And Salva?

He's definitely *the one*; he's on a Distinguished genetic line diverse enough from ours that our children will be uber-hot and though he's broken a few hearts, he's done so with poise and dignity. Yep, *it* definitely would have happened sometime this summer, if grandmother hadn't died. Now we'll have to wait till I'm back, though by the way he's pressing himself against me, I suspect Salva is not that interested in the waiting.

(Though he'll hardly take me here, right? Simply wouldn't be appropriate. Not with everybody waiting.)

"Stay," he says and it is neither suggestion or wish. It is a command. I tremble as his fingers brush through my hair. Only with me (for me!) does Salva ever reveal his boyish side. He's too young to shoulder all the responsibilities he does, to helm his company; his father's death was an accident, though not undeserved, karmically. Judging from the rumors I've heard (and from a few conversations with Salva on the topic) the man was distant and unkind. Salva's company is in better hands now, though I worry at the burden my love now carries.

I press against him.

"Mr. Durand, we must not disobey the most powerful woman in the world."

He smiles crookedly. "I'm increasing market share daily. Gehum Inc. will soon be more profitable than Terrasta Corp."

I grin. "Not if Viv has any say in it." My older sister is not fond of second place. Which, I suppose, is why she was born first.

Salva makes a show of shuddering, as if the mere mention of my sister horrifies him. I press my lips against his neck, not quite kissing him.

"Wait till she sees our nextgen modifications," he says, "they are out of this world."

Terrasta Corp. focuses on genetic modification of agriculture (crops and other boring shit). Gehum is on the other side of the spectrum, specializing in tweaking embryos so that children meet their parent's and society's expectations. Gehum is the reason why, in my generation, eighty-nine percent of all the girls have dark hair and skin, emulating a popular actress from my mother's generation.

One day his company might surpass Terrasta but that doesn't matter to me. I'll benefit either way because I intend for him to marry me.

"You'll have to show me, when I get back," I say.

He shrugs, pulling away, leaving me alone and confused.

"Maybe," he says, staring at the wall and the posters on it as if by studying them he'll come to a better understanding of me. "I might be busy. When you get back."

His affection is gone; I've insulted him. Time to stroke ego.

"I know your work is important… what is it you always say? Humans are like weeds, kudzu, ever growing and…."

"Never relenting, always pushing," he says, "our thirst for change is unquenchable. In the future, humans won't even…." His words trail off but the fire in his eyes does not dim. Even if I don't understand his fascinations I admire the passion they stir. He respects me enough that he never gets too carried away.

"Your mother knows how… miserable that planet is," he says. "Why is she dragging all of you with her?"

I shrug. It is ridiculous, us accompanying her. Sure, maybe Big Sister should, since she wants to be the boss one day, but the rest of us? Salva smiles and I think if I were any other gal in the universe I'd have melted then and there.

"I'll miss you, like you cannot imagine."

"I don't know about that. I have a rather active imagination, Miranda."

I flush, fumbling for words, for a proper

reply.

"Miranda Terrasta!"

I jump as a mahogany hued disc floats into the room. The ball-sized robot is our family's doser, dispensing our daily medications and though Adira might have remembered its full designation I do not (Adira is something of a know-it-all and there's no stopping her from spouting off facts, short of gagging, which is more or less illegal).

I just call the robot Doser.

"Tell bossy I'm on my way," I say.

Salva is glaring at the robot but also backing towards the window where presumably a glider or floater is waiting for him. *Presumably* because even Salva could not have flown up here on his own.

Before he reaches the window I lunge and pull him into a kiss, hoping Doser is recording every second of it with that intrusive camera eye of his. I think maybe for the first time ever I've flustered Salva because his exit through the window is clumsier than I'm sure he intends.

Before I'm able to chide the robot, he says, "There's a difference between kissing and licking, you'd do well to learn it."

I'm in a rocket ship, I tweet but I don't bother reading replies, snapping my phone closed instead. Unlike the old rockets of our almost forgotten past we sit horizontally, like a proper airplane, several stacked discs of passenger compartments filling the rocket, with a spiral staircase connecting floors.

Our family occupies the highest platform, below the cockpit. Plush red carpet covers the floor and velvet padding adorns the walls. The twins are talking to mother, Adira, and Viv (the three share a row of seats as far from mine as I could manage).

Finishing their goodbyes the twosome head towards me, passing several empty rows.

"Excited, sis?" Marcus asks. He's tall like us girls, with coffee brown skin and dark hair and light blue eyes. The twins are sixteen years old (a year older than Adira and a year younger than me) and they resemble everybody else in our generation (at least everybody whose parents loved them enough to indulge them, genetically). Yet Marcus and his twin, Junira, are also aberrations.

Twins are seldom born and their arrival into our high profile family was not unnoticed. Somebody had really screwed up in Gehum's labs, doubly so, because mother, ages ago, had declared that there would never be a male in our family again.

(And yeah, I don't know the story behind that. Nor why she choose to leave the twins home. When I asked mother earlier, why, she replied *"because"*. Which, isn't really ever an answer to anything.)

"Trade you places," I tease, knowing how much my brother wants to travel through space and how much Junira fears it.

"I think not," Junira says, "but don't worry, I'll find *something* to keep me entertained here."

"Oh, don't start that," Marcus says but I'm already leaning forward in my seat. Junira and I are, to use mother's parlance, peas in a pod. She — of all the others — is most like me. Fashionable and keen and always gorgeous. Yet we've never hit it off. She and Marcus were inseparable children, which according to the spin doctors on the web, is one of the reasons we bred twins out of our genetic profiles. They form unhealthy attachments to each another.

It would have been nice to have a sister to do my hair or to shop with (things neither Adira or Viv are well suited to). Nicer still if Junira's eyes wouldn't light up whenever she sees Salva.

"Behave yourself, June," I say. She smiles and moves on, patting my shoulder, about as much affection as a Terrastan ever displays.

"Ignore her." Marcus watches his twin depart. "She's teasing. She knows how you feel about Mr. Durand. We all know... you are never as subtle as you think."

"Mother too?" Not that I care. What does it matter? It is not like I'm shopping outside my district, choosing an unregistered genetic freak, a commoner. Salva is Distinguished, of quality breeding, and our alliance will bring more to the family than all of Viv's business acumen.

"Mother? She might be a genius but she's blind... to the important stuff." There's a trace of sadness in his voice that he doesn't even try hiding. I place my hand on his arm, I don't ask,

14

I don't pry.

"I'm okay. You'll be too. You're tougher than you think, Miranda."

And then my brother is off and I'm alone. I set my phone inside my purse and wait for the inevitable lift off, reminding myself that there is nothing to worry about. Our mother is practically a goddess. I smile at that thought, closing my eyes.

We are on our way to Grandmother's planet.

Just one stop, first.

CHAPTER 2

Meet the Crew

We are on the outer fringes of the inhabited solar system. Massive refineries drift past. They've been constructed from the mined and depleted shells of captured asteroids, joined via girders, to form entire orbiting communities. The asteroids, and the girders between them, are covered with webbing, thin biochemical strands capturing sunlight and converting it to energy. Human spiders crawl those webs.

All rather dull, if you ask me. Too much rock and steel. The only thing vaguely amusing is that more orbitals have Gehum's emblem painted on their sides than our Terrastan insignia. Tangible proof that my future husband is making the strides he claims.

A few of those orbitals are spacetowns, full of commoners willing to exchange the comforts of earth to do the actual grunt work of civilizing space. I don't understand why they bother.

"You still sulking, Merry?" Drea, my mother, asks as I stare out a viewport at the unending dreariness of space.

Mother floats beside me, wearing a t-shirt (untucked!) and joggers, like a lazy-ass commoner. My sisters are the same, as if being in space is some kinda excuse to run wild. I'm hoping nobody is vidrecording this, if my friends see my family's sloppy appearance in the tabloids there will be no end of my hearing about it.

"I'm not a child anymore." I'm neither edgy or snappy, I'm just speaking truth. Doser has increased all of our prescriptions for the voyage to help keep us civil.

"No, I suppose you are not."

The problem with being a middle child is that not only was I never *special* (neither the eldest with all her expectations and opportunities, or the youngest, spoiled and indulged, or even one of the twins, who are considered unique because they are not unique at all) I have never spent quality time alone with my mother. We don't know each other.

This is the first time in the two days we've spent traveling towards our initial stop that she's talked to me. The others are at the front, examining a wall-sized video screen displaying the map of grandmother's planet, as if actually excited. Doser hovers over Viv's shoulder.

I pretend to stare outside, as if lost in deep

thought (which I'm not) hoping mother will drift away. She does not.

"It is just a summer."

"*Just a summer*?" I blurt out; really who'd expect me to contain that? "Do you have any idea of what I'll be missing?" Dances and the beach; shopping and hanging out without cutting class. And that's not to talk about what Salva and I might have finally done! But mother can't understand any of these things so I tell her instead that there's more to life than her stupid company.

Thing is, mother has about as much control of her temper as I. "*Our* company feeds twenty billion people. *Our* company preserves the genetic stock of ninety percent of Earth's agriculture. Hardly stupid, Merry."

I glare at her. Mother inherited her position as CEO of Terrasta years before grandmother's death but she still lacks grandmother's flare in handling people. The two used to argue about whom had the most influence in the company's success, grandmother claiming it was her resourcefulness and business ability, mother, her genius with genetics. Mother had improved upon grandmother's initial terraforming of the planet and covered it with *old seed* to create a living vault that preserved original strains of plant life. Whenever the genetically modified crops of Earth (or those of the dozen colonies and hundreds of far flung orbitals that humanity has founded) falter, this vault can be used to restore them.

I think Viv will make a better CEO than either mother or grandmother.

"When we return to Earth," she says, "you'll have decisions to make. In regards to your future."

"Yeah, I guess."

"Are you thinking of working with us?"

"God, no!" I exclaim. What would my friends think if I became a scientist, or worse, a businesswoman?

"You are impossible."

"Hardly," I say. "Maybe I want to work elsewhere. Salva says he might find me an internship in Gehum's advertising department."

Mother purses her lips. "Salva Durand? How do you—"

"Our Merry knows everybody, mother."

I hadn't noticed Viv float up behind me and her presence (and voice) startles me from my handhold alongside the viewing window and I slip, floating away till Viv hauls me back to my perch. Can't say I've been much of a fan of gravity but its absence is a pisser.

Instead of thanking my sister I glare. Viv can't manage a minute being separated from mother. In the weak lighting my skin is almost sickly compared with theirs and though I'm thrilled not to have inherited their fashion sense, I do regret my paleness. I stand out like the Ugly Duckling from that classic vid.

"But Salva? He hardly swims in her circles," mother catches herself, realizing that I'm still (however reluctantly) part of this conversation,

"I mean to say, how did the two of you meet, Merry?"

Well that's a story in and of itself but it is not suitable for my mother. Viv flashes me a look and I'm wondering how much she knows. And I'm annoyed, at grandmother dying, at being forced to take this trip, at Viv's interruption. I want to be the bearer of good news; I want to bask in my mother's approval.

"We're dating mother. In fact, he came to visit me right before departure. That's why I was late." I say all this to mother but I'm staring at Viv. My older sister pretends not to care but she's only pretending, I know because she reaches and tugs her earlobe and she doesn't know she's doing it.

"Dating? That's... not right."

I blink. Mother should have been surprised, yes, but pleased too. "It is right; he's Distinguished and it is not like we are cousins."

(Our family has never mingled with Salva's.)

"A perfect match," I add.

"Perfect," mother whispers, not looking at Viv, which is unusual because the two share almost everything. She's staring at space like I was doing a moment earlier. "A perfect *genetic* union but hardly a proper match for you."

"You should be pleased," I say, tugging at my skirt. Such apparel is unwise in low gravity but I'm ingenious. Thin strips of Velcro join the hem to my leggings, keeping me modest and appropriate. "You *must* be pleased."

"The worst mistake your grandmother ever

made was giving Salva's grandfather access to Terrasta," she says, referring to grandmother's planet and not our company, "You may love any person in all the world, all the galaxy, but not him, not anybody from that dreadful family."

Viv appears as shocked as I. If there's a family as respected as ours, it is the Durands.

"Well I hardly care what you say. I love him and that's that."

Mother and I might have argued more but Adira interrupts us.

"Mother! Look!"

We can't see what she is seeing from our tiny window but that's all right because Adira taps the wall and fills the viewscreen she had been studying earlier with a view from the cameras mounted on the front of the shuttle. Our intermediary destination, a longhauler, fills the screen, a great spear of metal cast adrift in space. Lights sparkle up and down its length, from the narrow point at its front to the bulbous rear where water and volatiles are carried in a series of corrugated spheres.

A shuttle is not capable of *jaunting*. We'll use the longhauler instead, a journey of several hundred years compressed into no more than a month.

"What are those?" Viv asks. She's not talking about the longhauler. There are smaller specks of metal between us and the longhauler.

"Fighter craft," Adira says, "at least a dozen of them."

"It seems," mother murmurs, "that we have an escort."

I don't really care whether a few extra ships are coming with us. But I'm trying very hard not to be mortified by my family's behavior in front of any strangers that might be monitoring the cameras, especially any commoners, who, we all know, gossip far more than they should about matters above them. Images of us Terrasta gals in shabby clothing is not something I want broadcast.

It takes some muttering but I convince my uncouth family to dress more appropriately and we are almost civilized, in appearance at least, when we lock to the longhauler and enter the umbilical tunnel joining the ships. The outer lock rolls into place with a thud. The inner lock does not open.

Viv glances at mother, frowning.

"Just protocol," mother says though she's not looking at any of us, she's staring at her phone, instead. A datalink connection shouldn't exist out here but what do I know, right? She's mother after all.

It is back to waiting again and I'm well informed that I'm insufferable at it. The seconds trickle into minutes.

"Advertising now, is it?" Viv whispers to me and I clench my jaw, "wasn't it just last month that you and SueSal were going to open a fashion boutique—"

"Shut it," I mutter. Bad enough that I had made up the whole possibility of interning with Gehum to impress mother; I don't need it to backfire.

"You are too silly, too frivolous, fluttering like a hummingbird from flower to flower," Viv chides.

"A what?"

"Lord, Miranda, do you know anything?" Viv continues with her lecture but I stop listening, kicking off from the floor instead, with more force than I intend, drifting farther than I should, close to slamming into the opposite wall of the small waiting chamber. I stare at the white wall a couple minutes before Adira separates from Viv and lands beside me. I brace for the next part of the lecture, while wondering if mother really, really, needs all four daughters. If anybody would mind my disposing of the two accompanying us.

"Never mind Viv, she's jealous."

I blink, then double blink, at this uncharacteristic display of verbosity. Unless she's relating some pointless fact or another, Adira's never much of a speaker, especially when it involves being sympathetic, even more when it involves being sympathetic to me.

"She and Salva, when you were her age." Adira does something with her hands which I'm not sure is polite. I almost blush; she does. Viv watches us and I try to hide my surprise at Adira betraying our eldest sister's confidence. I'm impressed but don't know what to say. A

23

thank you will have to suffice.

"Maybe," Adira says, "when you are done with him, it'll be my turn? Seems a family tradition."

Now I really don't know what to say but I'm smiling and she's smiling and then she's drifting back to mother. She doesn't look at me again, just shoves her nose into her tablet, reading the latest on whatever subjects have caught her interest. I know everybody's always saying there's more to people than what you see, that they can surprise you, but I've never believed it until now.

Still I'm not amused long. The waiting gives my thoughts ample time to creep forward and torment me. Salva and Viv? He conveniently forgot to mention this to me and though we're not sleeping together, this should have come up at some point, right? And now I'm wondering about Junira. If Salva were any other man I would not have put it past him to seduce all the women of house Terrasta. But he's not that man.

I'm tormenting myself over this, wondering whether I should feel betrayed (after all, it happened long ago, right... not relevant now), when Doser suggests that there has been a malfunction.

"A what?" Viv barks, as loud as the robot, who, in his infinite kindness rattles on about how umbilical airlocks occasionally fail to open properly, spilling the occupants into space. He even has statistics to back him up. Luckily (for us) the robot is wrong and the inner lock does eventually roll open, revealing the crew.

There's a lull as we stare at the four crewmen. Last summer I organized a ball with the theme of space travel and learned to read rank insignias. The tallest man, who'd have been handsome if he wasn't so old (mid thirties and growing a beard that hasn't been in style since my mother was a baby) is the captain, despite the wrinkles in his blue coat. The two gray coated men behind him, both younger and with fewer adornments on their lapels, are low ranking pilots. Slightly off to the side of the three military men is an engineer wearing a black tunic over white trousers.

Meeting the engineer's gaze I realize mother is making a mistake but not in time to stop her. When two groups are introduced there is a formal process that must always be observed (to avoid embarrassment). The highest ranking individual must be the first to address the other party. So, mother (because mother outranks everybody in the galaxy) must introduce herself first, but to the highest ranking member of the other party. Which mother, in her social denseness, misperceives to be the captain.

"Thank you for allowing us aboard," mother says, waving her hand towards us, her daughters, introducing us one by one. Viv and Adira are graceful in their responses but both repeat mother's mistake, focusing their attention on the captain.

I do not. I angle myself, so that my

respectful nod is directed at both the captain and the engineer, whom I've perceived as being Distinguished. This makes his superiority over the rest of the crew, whom I am certain are commoners, guaranteed. I finish my response and the captain shuffles, awkward. Because mother greeted him first he ought to be the first to respond but he hesitates long enough to let the Distinguished man have the honor.

"Engineer Johann, of the *Deckers*." The engineer puts the appropriate emphasis on his family name and immediately I place him; he's even been to the same ball or two as me, though he's several years older and out of my scope of interest. He's handsome, dark of skin and hair (of course), with deep, hazel eyes.

He introduces the rest of the men. Captain Jennings, the pilot, a Mr. Tring, and the co-pilot, Mr. Fowler. A round of respectful inquiries, meaningless in their wording but fundamental to building a solid foundation of propriety between us, occurs, before the serious discussion is reached.

"Please accept my apologies, for the delay," Captain Jennings says. "Our *escort* would not permit us to commence boarding until they verified your identities."

"We accept your apologies," I say before mother speaks; I know she would forget the entire accepting of the apology which would be guaranteed to manifest an awkwardness between both parties for the entire duration of the voyage.

Mother casts me a funny look (she is quite oblivious) and asks, "And why, captain, do we have such an impressive escort?"

The captain says, "The fighters came direct from Gehum. Mentioned precious cargo."

Decker casts me an amused gaze and I have the breeding to blush. Salva has lent us these starfighters, to protect us... protect me? Flattering enough that I (almost) decide to set aside the whole matter of his dipping wick with Viv.

"Come, let us show you to your quarters," Decker says, "and at dinner, tonight, we have a delightful surprise."

"What do you suppose the surprise is?" I ask, after we are settled, each in a bedroom that I'd have been embarrassed to show my friends but sufficiently superior to the cramped confines of the shuttle. We have a common room, with three low couches and a video console, to ourselves. We've primped and preened and are ready for dinner.

Like the others, my hair is rolled into a tight bun; the longhauler as lacking in gravity as the shuttle and I'd rather not have my long hair snagged when an automatic door closes. Worst thing in all the world for me would be to lose my hair, which if unrestrained, flows past my waist.

Dinner can't come soon enough, as far as I'm concerned. Just seeing Viv is a constant reminder of Salva and her — and yeah, I've watched enough primetime to readily fuel my imagination, in regards to what the two of them did. And I really don't care to be snared into any more conversations with mother. Some battles we never win.

"Why would anybody with a sane mind want to waste their time mucking about with humans when there is more important work to be done, elsewhere," mother says, obviously referring to my earlier discussion though pretending she's addressing all of us. Mother has mastered these subtle digs; if she wasn't a genetic and botanical genius I suppose she could've taught a class on passive aggressiveness.

I roll my eyes.

"I agree, mother," Viv says, "ensuring we have adequate and diverse crops, seems an infinitely more honorable pursuit than Gehum's genetic tampering."

Better if I had waited for dinner in my bedroom but it is unseemly for me not to be here, with them. With nothing else to do I decide to piss mother off.

"Salva says that when he's done revolutionizing Gehum, all of your crops will become irrelevant," I declare. These are the kinds of discussions he and I have, late at night huddled around our phones. Yeah, I know the content of our conversations lacks a certain romance but he's so passionate about his responsibilities that be assured they are not lacking in spark.

"You should understand," Viv says, "that what Salva — and his father before him — have attempted, is nothing short of monstrous. The way Gehum modifies humans is—"

"Hypocrite!" I cry, "we are all modified."

"We are *tweaked*," Viv says, "simple manipulations. When we return to Earth you'd do yourself a favor if you reviewed the patent applications Gehum has filed over the years. Then you'd understand. Salva has no intention of just modifying humans... he wants to create new species."

I shrug, this not being entirely news to me. There's world of difference between breeding humans with a certain hair color, skin tone, and doing some of what Salva has suggested. Humans who don't eat, who need only sunlight for subsistence; humans capable of surviving underwater or in the vacuum of space.

Far-fetched and far-future kinds of things. But still I'm annoyed that they've twisted his intent and I promise myself I'll never let them bait me again. Nobody wins an argument when mother and Viv are on the opposing team.

When Mr. Decker arrives to escort us to dinner I'm sure he senses the hostility between us but is gentlemanly enough not to comment on it. We drift down the corridors, all of us struggling to keep our gowns from floating away on us as we trail him.

"You must accept my apologies for the amusement ahead," he says, stopping us outside the red painted doors to the dining hall. There's more crew, almost twenty to keep the ship functioning, but we've not seen them yet. Which is as it should be.

"Amusement?" Viv asks; at some point she has taken up a position to Decker's side and I suppose that is of no consequence. Not improper at all, if she is showing interest in him. They'd be a fine match and Viv probably should marry before she inherits Terrasta.

"Your robot should remain outside," he says and though we all exchange curious glances we concede.

"Do not blame the captain," Decker says, "for it was my idea to surprise you. I hope that after your initial shock you'll appreciate the gesture; after all it is difficult to find cause for true and novel surprise in our society."

"I really don't understand," Viv says but then he is opening the door and there's really no further reason for words.

"Oh my," I whisper, doing my best to hide my surprise, far exceeding the effort of Adira, who's staring as if one of her books has come alive before her very eyes, and Viv, my big sister, is less restrained.

She faints.

Chapter 3

A Traveling Zoo

Mr. Decker is swift and catches Viv but I barely notice because a muscular savage sits at the head of our dining table. His blond hair falls past his shoulders, the hair as mesmerizing as the man. I've never seen a shade like it before, except in historicals about commoners. And none of those men had the savage's *presence*.

Both the savage and the captain (who is seated to the savage's left) rise as we enter. The savage is too bulky for the tunic he's wearing, his chest and arms rippling beneath the fabric. He's not as tall as Mr. Decker but his build is robust; solid and muscular.

"Good evening," the captain says as Mr. Decker sets Viv gently into her seat.

"Ladies," Decker says, "I introduce Kal Rothson."

"But he's… he's a…." Viv mutters, still

flustered.

"A Promoted, yes," Mr. Decker says.

"It is my pleasure," the savage, says, "to make your acquaintances." His accent is almost musical.

A round of greetings ensue, and we all settle into chairs, the ladies conglomerating on one end of the reasonably sized table, the men on the other. It would not be appropriate for any of the other crew to be dining with us at our first meal.

I know some of my friends follow the comings and goings of the Promoted with as much eagerness as lower classes follow my family's movements, but I've always disliked this bit of showmanship from Gehum. Plucking ripe fruit from Terrasta, *our* planet, and parading them around the galaxy, showing us *man in his primitive form*.

No better than a traveling zoo. And I understand now why Doser was made to stay outside. There are certain precautions that must be taken. We expose Kal to a limited subset of our technology because he will be forced to live the remainder of his miserable life back on that primitive world. Too cruel for him to see how wondrous our universe is.

I glance up from where I've settled my gaze on the tablecloth velcroed to the table (there are no plates of course, our food will be served in plastic tubes) and I see that Kal watches me, as he fields questions from my mother. Beneath his wide eyes and ready grin, there's a hardness.

Not anything threatening, just the promise of potential violence. He is a man of action. The captain and Mr. Decker, both fit men, are rendered insignificant beside Kal.

There's more than that too. His gaze, it makes me uncomfortable.

"And your rank in the tribe?" Adira asks, kinda surprising me because she doesn't even have her tablet in hand, to make notes.

"I will succeed my father as headman of the *clan*. If my brother doesn't kill me before then."

The three of us, our mother's daughters, all blanch and somehow, instinctively, we glance at Drea Terrasta. She's smiling and staring at Kal with the same intensity as Kal has been staring at me.

"He's kidding. Things are not so terrible down there."

Kal nods but he presses his lips together and looks away, off to the side, as if able to see his homeland through the hull.

"Conditions are far from bliss, however," he says, drumming the table with his fingers. "The wild herds are plentiful and we have ample food but the… skies are loud, full of thunder. The stormcurse floods our valleys with relentless rain."

"Rain?" I had no intention of joining the conversation but am prompted to do so now. It has to be noted that I hate rain.

"The wet is rotting the forests."

Mother shakes her head. "The readings, I've taken, on the remote instruments, hasn't shown more than a slight increase in precipitation, the past few decades." She takes a sip from a bulb of coffee that a servant has brought into the room. (Servants, though rare, are even more invisible to me than robots.)

"You do not see what you think you see," Kal says. Mother's knuckles whiten as she tightens her grip on her bulb.

"Mr. Rothson has been absent for several years," Mr. Decker says, "and much has probably changed since his departure."

The broad shouldered man shrugs. "We will know soon enough."

What's the point of having a rich family, I think. Bad enough that I'm dragged across the universe to grandmother's planet, but I really don't think I deserve to waste my summer being rained on. I slump into my seat, now, officially, having even less interest in going to Terrasta.

After dinner we return to our cabins and mother heads to her bed chambers, but me and my sisters can't sleep, our minds too wired over what has happened. So engrossed are we in talking about the shock of being trapped with a savage, none of us notice the longhauler shudder as we push through the first gate and tunnel across time and space, several hundred lightyears in an eye blink, throwing ourselves from Official Space into the Uncharted Territory.

We'll jaunt through several of these gates to

traverse the universe, until we reach the system where Terrasta orbits a bright yellow sun. Terrasta is grandmother's discovery and it is our family's property, our world. Other companies, like Gehum, pay us for the privilege of using Terrasta's resources.

The three of us are seated around a small table, our feet on it, our gowns floating as if caught by a perverse breeze. My stomach growls, the processed food is unappetizing, nothing like the feasts we enjoy back on Earth: homemade pastas and breads and lean meats, all of it possible because of mother's crops, because of Terrasta's seeds. If there's one consolation about reaching our destination it is that we'll resume eating properly.

"He's a grotesque beast," Viv says, before slipping the straw of her juice bulb back into her mouth.

I shudder, thinking of Kal's muscular body, caged in clothing cut for another man's build, and how his eyes had inappropriately fallen upon me, looked through me, as if dismissing me of my clothing (and dignity!) in one sweeping gaze.

Shocking enough that we are to spend our time in the presence of many commoners but Kal, being here... almost unthinkable. Even unforgivable. But I'm already anticipating my friend's reactions when I return home. The stories I'll tell. Nothing that happens to them over summer will come close to matching my dining with a Promoted on his way home (I might not like the concept of bringing savages to Earth, as entertainment, but my friends do).

"It is strange, isn't it," Adira says, "that nobody, not even mother, knew about his being aboard?"

"Kind of like the fighter escort," Viv adds. "Mother should have known that too."

It is unnerving to realize mother doesn't have quite the same authority in space as she does on Earth. For my two sisters I think it is worse because they worship Drea Terrasta in a way I never will.

"I'm surprised Salva's being so… pompous," Adira murmurs.

I glare at her. "He's not pompous!"

My sister grins back, at my response.

Viv snorts. "You don't think he sent those fighters here, for you?" I blush, because yes, I do. "He's just demonstrating to mother that Gehum is capable of supporting their own fleet."

Adira adds, "That would have been unthinkable a few years ago." Our company dominates space, has a monopoly; mother owns almost ninety percent of all active space vehicles. But I don't want to talk about any of that and I do such an epic eyeroll that even Viv laughs.

"Fine, Miranda. Tell me instead, what you think of Johann."

I'm well pleased that my big sister recognizes that I'm a better judge of people than the rest of them, but even in the privacy of our quarters

I'm uncomfortable with straying so far from etiquette. "Mr. Decker appears to be a standard example of a man of fine breeding. Proud, with just enough arrogance to make him entertaining, not so much as to be insufferable. And he has a sense of humor, which is often lacking in men."

"And he's yummy," Adira adds. Viv grins and we talk more, even gossiping about the pilots. I've never enjoyed being around my sisters but this isn't so terrible. As we share our yawns, weary and ready for slumber, I admit I'm (almost) enjoying myself.

But I can't shake Kal from my thoughts. It is not that I am attracted to him — I admit I am, to a degree, as would any woman, for he is handsome and exotic and there is no denying the inherent desirability of those traits — but it is like his presence here is a signal, a movement in an intricate and foreign dance, the steps to which I am oblivious. I don't know the next move.

I say, "At least we won't see much of him."

To keep Kal from being exposed to the miracles of our modern world, we'll only visit with him during meals; Mr. Decker is his handler on this, the return leg of Kal's journey, and it will fall to him to make sure Kal does not return to Terrasta contaminated by our culture.

The days pass. I'm not sleeping well; weightlessness and I do not mix, I suppose. I'm half tempted to trim my hair, for it somehow unravels itself during the night cycle and I find myself chewing on it when I wake. The nightmare's don't help either.

It is always Salva in them, floating outside my bedroom window. He says nothing, does nothing, just watches me. I wake most mornings trembling and covered in sweat as if I've spent the night being chased by hordes of mindless zombies. Makes no sense

I keep busy. Every jaunt station has a data pumper, an unmanned orbital that is updated with all the content from Earth's world wide web. It is always a few days behind but it lets me keep up with what is going on in the world. I upload my replies to my friend's queries to a pumper, knowing that an Earthbound ship will bring the data back home and synchronize it with the great hive mind of the human species. Everybody will know which comments they've made that I've liked and which have displeased me. Life continues.

I download new music tracks and sometimes I dance by myself, imagining my vidfeed is live, all my friends dancing with me, like normal. Other times I listen to the music and pull images from the Web onto my tablet, scrapping them onto various boards and using my light pen to alter them. I'm thinking about leveraging my shares in Terrasta and developing my own business. I'm going to start with gowns, I think. I work on designs and fill my tablet with them, as we grow ever nearer to our destination.

Without the constant chatter of social media

I am lonely beyond the pale but I am also active and occupied and if not for the inadequate sleepage, I think I'd be almost satisfied. But today my shoulders are aching and I'm bored, tired of sitting alone in my room, tablet propped on my knees. I dismiss my music and slip out, my skirt ruffling, the Velcro on it is wearing thin and I'm having a harder time convincing it not to float away on me. If I were more practical I'd wear trousers, like my sisters and mother, but I'm still a lady, space travel or not. Skirts are fashionable; pants are not. And that's all there is to it.

This afternoon I pass by mother's door, using the drift handles to pull myself along. I knock but mother ignores me; she and Adira spend their time inside mother's suites (converted into a makeshift lab where she's busy analyzing data). I don't know why she doesn't just wait. On Terrasta we'll be living at the landing site (cleverly known as Landing) in a complex built on an island far away (and hidden) from the savages inhabiting the main continent. Mother will have access to her state of the art laboratory there and we'll at least have the creature, if not social, comforts our rank entitles us to.

I don't bother with Viv's room. Several times she has sneaked into our quarters well past sleep shift; Mr. Decker and her have found a more satisfying way to pass the long spaceflight, I imagine. I think he's become more than an amusement for her. We'll have to see.

I'd be happy for her if she wasn't such a bitch.

At least Viv won't have to worry about any *complications*. Weeks before the flight from Earth we started taking supplements to shut down our menstrual cycle. Though done primarily as a convenience — space travel not offering much to recommend it in the areas of hygiene — the supplements are also birth control. Viv and Mr. Decker can dip wick as often as they want without worrying over the repercussions. Not that birth control is hard to find back on Earth but us Terrastan gals always have to be careful about the medication we take, since medical records (even ours!) are publicly accessible. The media loves to announce when the rich and the famous start on birth control, as if it is proof that we are behaving improperly.

The captain allows us access to the main bridge (not that he can really refuse, I suppose) and I figure I might as well spend an hour or two there. I pass several commoners and am rather proud of myself. I neither flinch nor look away as they smile at me. A couple times I even return their *hellos*. Our dinners usually include only us gals, the captain, Kal and Mr. Decker; other times there is a wider range of crew. I've grown more accustomed to the commoners. After all it is not their fault, their parents simply couldn't afford to give them a proper genetic inheritance. It might make them unsuitable for friendship or more, but they are still people, more or less. I'm learning more about myself every day, learning that I can be gracious to those beneath me.

Kal, the Promoted, he is another story. Not a single cell in his body has ever been tweaked; he is a *wild seed*, like an uncultivated plant, never pruned or fertilized. His body is a random collection of cells, with no inherent order or purpose. I don't shudder or think of Kal as inherently evil (after all I don't belong to any of those new churches that promote genetic inferiority as the work of the Devil, we Terrastans are still proud, if rather nonpracticing, Catholics). Kal is just a savage and for that he deserves my pity.

The bridge is set about dead center on the rectangular longhauler and juts from the top, overlooking the rest of the starship. I climb the metal ladder leading into it. We are in-between jaunts, so I see a glorious display of stars. There's a single jaunt remaining before we arrive in Terrasta's system; a few days away from what I'm sure will be the worst summer vacation of my life.

The bridge is empty; nobody sits in the captain's chair or the pilot's chair and even the copilot and navigator seats are vacant. I look around, not concerned because the crew carries mobiles; they control the ship as effectively from the lavatory as from here. I pause at the top and sigh, reveling in the thrum of machinery, computers everywhere, just like back home. Behind the hole where the ladder enters the room is a stack of three crates screwed to the wall. Spare supplies, the pilot told me earlier, so that the crew can make quick repairs.

"In case we are attacked by aliens." He had said this with a short-lived grin, but was soon dumbfounded by my blank look. He tried explaining that in old science fiction vids every time a ship was attacked all the computers on the bridge would erupt into smoke. He was trying to make a joke that I'm still not certain I understand. Unless the bridge was hit directly by an alien attack (an imaginary alien attack, since there are no aliens, unless you count men like the Promoted) why would the computers be damaged? And if the bridge were hit, wouldn't everybody there, die?

(I know some dorks like the classics but I've never understood the appeal.)

"While I am enjoying the view; I'd rather like to enter," a stern voice says from below. "The bridge, that is."

I blush, recognizing Kal's voice. I want more than anything to climb down and flee but the ladder is the only entrance, only exit. If I continue standing here, my skirt billowing around my waist, he'll continue to have his view of my underwear. I move.

I'm red in the face and desperate not to make eye contact as the savage joins me on the bridge. He makes no move to step away from the ladder hole, to allow my escape.

"It appears," Kal says, with a hungry grin, "that we are alone."

CHAPTER 4

Alone With a Savage

This is beyond all propriety.

"Where's Mr. Decker?" My back is pressed against the smooth contours of a terminal.

"Oh, he takes his dog off his rope, once in a while," Kal says. But he is merciful and moves aside, towards the opposite side of the small bridge. He settles into the navigator's vacant chair.

Is it possible that Kal realizes the situation he has put me in and recognizes my discomfort? If so it is unexpected, and more to the point, against everything and anything I have heard about the men of Terrasta.

"Thank you."

His crosses his thick, muscular arms and I can't stop myself from biting my lips. A man like Salva conveys his power by the sheer force of his personality, and by implication, the resources he has at his command. Kal is all physicality, a looming, figure, a contrast to the thin and angular men of my world and more like those archetypal heroes from the kid's morning programs the robots used to set me in front of during childhood.

"You expected worse from me?" There's a flush to his light skin.

"I didn't," I lie. "But what, you said, looking up my—"

"If you wore trousers, like your sisters, I would've had nothing to look at."

"You can hardly fault me for that. Should I dress like a man because I'm trapped here…."

"Trapped," he says, chewing on the word. There's a glimmer in his eyes and I'm not sure if I'm frightened or intrigued. "That's what you are, a prisoner?"

"No, of course not." I remember that he's not to know more than he should about our society. He cannot bring ideas back with him that might *advance* his own primitive state. I ponder that, having never really pondered it before. How awful it must be for the Promoted who return to their planet after seeing all the wonders of our civilization.

"I am not a monster," he says.

"But you must understand my concern." My heart does not thud quite so hard now (or at least not for the same reason as before).

"I did not choose this. I did not ask to be taken from my clan and brought here."

I make a face. He might protest but what

man wouldn't want to have lived Kal's life the past few years? He has enjoyed countless parties and extravaganzas in his honor. Surely this has more than made up for the rounds of genetic testing and sampling and extraction!

As Salva explains it the Promoted's genetic offerings are analyzed and woven into our every generation's genes, a layer of genetic robustness without which our society (which runs the risk of sameness) might face extinction from a virulent strain of virus or some other danger that exploits genetic similarities. Even commoners, free of charge, are thus improved.

It is much the same reason we keep pure plant strains on Terrasta. If a blight develops on Earth that is capable of eradicating a particular crop, we are able to recover the seed from Terrasta and modify it to be resilient to the new danger. Our society has perfected balancing between diversity (which has advantages but is also chaotic and inefficient; not ideal characteristics when there are billions of mouths to feed) and our efficient, single sourced crops.

Of course there are many women, in our bored and privileged upper classes, who prefer a more direct *genetic sample*. Kal has not suffered from physical loneliness in his exile.

"I am sure your sufferings have been many."

He laughs. "I will never understand your world, where women are free to speak their minds."

"It is not your way?" I ask, cautious. Little is

45

known of their clans, or I should say I know little. I am sure there are anthropology geeks, like Adira, who drool as new tidbits of information from our manufactured savages roll in, insights into how past societies might have functioned and all that. But I don't waste my time with documentaries.

He shakes his head and glances at the great black expanse. "None of this fits with what I knew before. But as awesome as that," he pauses, pointing at the stars, "the idea that women rule men… this I shall never speak of with my clan."

He smiles, almost shyly, at the admission and then studies me a moment before continuing, "Miranda, do you know how I came to be Promoted?"

I blink, startled by this abrupt change in discussion. I shake my head and he pushes himself from the chair and vaults across the bridge to land beside me. I flinch, at his proximity. I smell him, feel him; he's too imposing, too *there*.

"There is a cave near a place we call the Tower and it is where our peoples hold a festival. The clans come together, only the magicians know when, they being our time keepers. We hold this festival and it lasts all summer," he says. "Midway through, we enter the cave to be judged by our godlings."

Godlings? I almost laugh and I suspect if I were any of my sisters I might have, but though I do not know his customs I at least understand they are *customs* and ridiculing them (openly) is disrespectful. I nod and encourage him to continue.

"The godlings poke our flesh and feed from our blood. They decide which man will be chosen."

I realize this is how Salva's engineers at Gehum make their decision. The men's blood must be taken and analyzed during this ceremony. When Kal returns, another savage — from his clan or one of the others scattered across the planet — will be taken.

"But you haven't told me how they brought you away from your… lands. What was that like?"

He smiles. "I don't know. I was drunk. I entered the cave and the godling fed and I waited, beside our clan's magician, Veers, and he chanted and chanted and my eyelids fell shut and—"

"You woke up on a… vessel." I use his word for the longhauler.

"No," he admits, "I woke up, in your world. I came to understand I had been transported there, somehow, but I slept through the entire thing."

I suspect Kal should probably be asleep for the return voyage too. Why let him see space travel, now? Or has he been kept awake simply to amuse us? Decker's idea that, or Salva's?

"This must be… overwhelming."

He nods. "When I came aboard this vessel and met the captain I could not fathom a more powerful man. To have the power of traveling between worlds, this vessel at his command. But then your mother arrives and it is all turned on its head."

"It is our custom," I say.

He is not smiling as he stares at me. "More than that, I think. They treat her as if she is above and beyond, as if she is a great godling."

I can hardly deny that I've harbored similar thoughts and it surprises me that this primitive man shares my insight. Mother is powerful. We stare at each other and for the first time I'm thinking that he's not so formidable. That beneath the tough lines of his hardened muscles, muscles that have not grown soft despite his years of almost-captivity, there's sadness. Perhaps there is. Perhaps he has seen the wonders of a world and knows he will be denied them forever. Perhaps he is simply frightened.

But of my mother? She might be powerful but she's hardly a terrifying individual. Still, for no reason I'll ever understand, I settle my hand on his and squeeze.

A noise from below separates us, it would not do for either of us to be seen like this.

"Be safe," he says as he exits the bridge.

"He didn't!" Viv cries, fingers over her mouth as I relate what happened to me on the bridge earlier in the day.

We've arrived for dinner early and our table

is empty except for my sisters and I. Three of the six sidetables are filled with the pilots who man the fightercraft. We've seen them before. During jaunts their ships have to attach to the longhauler and the pilots stay inside, with us.

They avoid eye contact; they are commoners and they know it (though it hasn't kept us gals from gossiping about them and admiring their physical characteristics). If it were not for my loyalty to Salva I'd have considered a fling or two. But we're not talking about them now, my sisters are riveted by my description of the encounter with Kal.

"Did he touch you?" Adira whispers. I nod before I'm able to stop myself. Both grimace.

"Disgusting," Viv pronounces.

Adira adds, "He should be punished."

I'm about to protest but then Viv's eyes widen. "He… he didn't…."

"No." I utter a silent curse at my skin for its inability to hide a blush. And really… I can't say exactly why I am blushing. Sure Kal was inappropriate, and maybe I had been too, in touching him. But it was not as if it had been more than just a passing touch between two very different peoples for the briefest of moments.

"I'll talk to Mr. Decker tonight," Viv says. "Adira is right, there ought be a punishment."

It takes me several minutes to insist no punishment is necessary and that I'd rather forget the entire thing and gradually my sisters drop the issue, though it is clear they are apprehensive over Kal having dinner with us. Their fears turn out to be baseless for Kal does not accompany the captain.

"He's tired," Mr. Jennings explains, not meeting my gaze and not saying more and I fear perhaps that Kal has been punished anyways. If even just to be exiled from the rest of us.

Neither Mr. Decker or mother attend dinner that night and we eat with the captain. He takes care not to speak, except to answer our queries, which are few, for we have dined with him too often to have much more to wonder about. And none of us, despite our curiosity, bring up Kal's absence.

After dinner the captain bids us good night and adds. "Our journey is almost at an end and tomorrow we begin preparations for landing."

"So soon?" Adira asks.

He nods. "Yes, we'll enter the system close enough to Terrasta to begin our approach. In a couple days your family will enter quarantine. This might be our last dinner together; things will be busier for me."

I lead my sisters in being polite and thanking him for his hospitality. The longhauler will remain in orbit until the end of summer but shuttles will only land a few times; once to drop us off and another excursion to pick us back up. Kal will return to his people on a separate trip. Any supplies being sent down to Landing will be drop shipments, from orbit, to avoid the expense of fueling return craft.

For the two months we are on the planet

we'll be separated from the rest of the universe. Which means, I realize, as I enter our quarters, that the minimal correspondence I've maintained with Salva (exchanging emails and texts) will also end.

I want to give Salva something more, so he doesn't forget me. I will use Doser's cameras to record a video message and send it, before we land. One last message so that my love will remember me. And maybe, I think, reminded of Kal's presence, so I do not forget Salva.

CHAPTER 5

Almost There

Two days after my strange meeting with Kal, I attempt to finish my message to Salva.

Hi, Salva. I really… really miss you! I want—

"Erase that one," I tell Doser. Too sentimental and beneath mine and Salva's relationship. I'm sitting cross-legged on my bed, prettied up as best as I can muster given the bleakness of the longhauler, and staring into the robot's camera.

Hello, Mr. Durand. I hope this message finds you well and not too exhausted from your work. Please forgive my shabby appearance; I am doing my best. You should see how horrid my sisters look. Viv even—

Damn, I think, biting my lip. I probably shouldn't mention my sister, that'll only remind him that he's bedded her and not me and that can't possibly be healthy for our relationship.

"Again?" Doser asks, and in his modulated voice, I detect annoyance. Or perhaps it is only an echo of my frustration. This one way conversation is more difficult than talking to Salva directly. Not that he is ever an easy man to communicate with.

"Yes. Erase it. We'll get it right, eventually."

"Preferably before we land."

"Shut it, robot," I snap. I realize Doser requires a higher degree of independence than, say, the robot back home that used to toast my bread, but I doubt he needs to be such a prick to perform his duties reliably.

He toots, distastefully.

"Let's get this over with," I say.

Hello, Mr. Durand. I hope this message finds you well and maybe, somehow, thinking of me a little. I know you are busy but I do have hopes that I occupy some of your thoughts, as you occupy mine. Perhaps you think I am silly. Does it shock you if I say I do not care? I know how I feel about you.

We will land soon and I'll lose even this tenuous contact between you and me. I do hope you have some pity, for this adventure my mother is forcing upon me.

Oh! And I've encountered one of your projects, though I suspect you already know about him, that you were involved in his being here. We were all suitably disgusted by his presence.

But... he's interesting too, I suppose. I understand why you say that working with humans is more satisfying than mother's crop tinkering. Plants don't have stories to tell, or sadness in their eyes, or anything else that merits real interest.

Oh... anyways. The flight's been a real bore. I thought maybe my... family and I might get along better but we haven't. Anyways, Mr. Durand, I miss you and I am counting the days until we meet again.

Anyways, I guess we'll talk later. We'll have plenty of catching up.

After Doser tells me the message has been sent I resume packing. The longhauler is now in orbit around our planet. Soon we'll be transferred to the shuttle and then—

"What do you mean quarantine!" I hear Viv's voice coming from the living room and I pop my door open, Doser trailing me. My eldest sister is arguing with Mr. Decker and he's lost some of his composure, one hand tucked into his pocket as Viv drifts side to side. The low gravity equivalent of pacing, I suppose.

She's rather amusing looking, her hair unbound and trailing behind her like the fan of a peacock. I only wish it was not so curly and dark, making my own seem somehow lacking.

I vaguely remember the captain saying something about quarantine at our last dinner.

"It is required," Mr. Decker says.

"And isn't us being here, on this ship, quarantine enough, Johann?"

"It is painless, I promise."

Viv has more questions and her shouting eventually draws mother and Adira to the chamber but, thankfully, Mr. Decker flees before Viv overreacts and embarrasses us further. Twenty minutes later, we are ushered towards the airlock separating us from our shuttle.

The glowing panel beside the airlock door is red, meaning the door is locked. A smaller door beside it (that I haven't noticed before) has its panel lit green.

"It is like a shower," mother explains, "who wants to go first?"

"They can't see us, in there, can they?" Me, being ever practical, ask.

"Of course they can. They need to verify you've followed the instructions they'll give you. It is vital that there be no external, or internal, organisms, to contaminate Terrasta."

Now I flush. "I don't want—"

"My goodness, girls. An AI will do the actual viewing of the footage and dispose of it. No human eyes will ever see it. Now, grow up." She shoves Viv into the room, as if she is really this eager to land on the cursed planet. My sister relents, entering the tiny room and closing the door after her. About ten minutes later the door opens and I take my turn, not wanting to wait in the hall with my non-interactive family.

It is smaller than the closets inside my closet at home. There's a screen with instructions written on it and I'm sure behind that screen is the nefarious camera.

The first instruction is to undress and to place my clothing in the metal bin before me. I do this, though it takes longer for me than for my sister as I'm layered. First comes the knee high white leather boots, the last the lace cap I've woven into my hair (which I wouldn't have wasted my time doing, if I had known about this). Eventually I'm naked and shivering, drifting from foot to foot on the cold metal plating which I've just now realized is a grate, like the walls and ceiling. I'm trying my hardest not to brush against the sterile, steel walls.

The instruction changes, the camera or robot or whatever, obviously determining I'm naked now. I'm really hoping that none of the crew are looking at this footage and I'm hard pressed not to cover myself with my hands.

Now the screen is telling me to stand still. Which is kind of funny given that standing is rather difficult, without gravity. I'm just smiling about that when nozzles erupt from each corner.

It is not exactly a shower. The fluid is cool, though warmer than the room itself, and as it splashes against my skin, I close my eyes instinctively. It doesn't feel like water though; it is thicker, gel-like. Fans whirl, sucking up the excess moisture, through the grates.

Then it stops, the gel drying almost instantaneously, and my eyes flicker open only to snap shut again, the room filled with a blinding blue light. Then an automated voice tells me it is over.

A hatch opens on the wall and there's fresh clothing. But not my clothing. Thick black trousers and a heavy green work shirt and even heavier black boots. Socks and goddamn granny panties to complete the ensemble.

If I were less modest I'd have staged a revolution right there but the thought of exiting the shower naked, makes that impossible. I dress instead and when I emerge I see that Viv wears the same outfit as I.

"Mother's choice," she explains and I don't think she's any more pleased than I. Mother hasn't tried dressing us in years. This must be some kind of late-life hormonal revenge. "What we were wearing is being shipped back to Earth, along with everything we packed."

"Are you serious?" I ask and she nods and I ask it again, once the others are through quarantine (though first I have to stop Adira from rattling on, she's excited and telling us the names of all the bugs and viruses and bacteria that have just been eradicated). I'm pissed that all my effort in planning a suitable wardrobe for this dreadful excursion has been wasted.

Mother even justifies her cruelty. "I've taken the liberty of choosing more appropriate clothing for all of you."

"But this is hideous!" Though my sisters and I seldom find common ground, we are united in this. We are dressed worse than commoners.

"Miranda, do you truly believe you'll have occasion to be wearing gowns on the planet?"

I had planned to stay close to the research facility at Landing. Had definitely not intended actually walking into the woods or anything horrible like that.

"Maybe," I say.

"You are an impossible child," mother says and then she walks past me, past us all, into the gray umbilical connecting us to the shuttle.

What choice do we have but to follow?

This shuttle is the opposite of the vessel that rocketed us away from Earth; small and spartan, the umbilical enters a single, cramped chamber, with only two rows of seats. My mother and sisters quickly fill the front row, leaving me to share the back with Kal.

I'm shocked to see him. He shouldn't be here; the first trip down was suppose to be just us gals. There's no sign of Mr. Decker yet, either, and given that he's responsible for Kal, that's odd too.

Kal smiles and says hello and I do the same as I sit, leaving an empty seat between him and I. I've not seen him since our encounter on the bridge but I've occasionally heard his voice through the doors of his quarters, laughing or otherwise engaged.

Through a small alcove in front of me I watch the pilot, Mr. Tring, man the shuttle's console. He detaches us from the longhauler, that massive ship seemingly pulling away from us at great velocity, though I realize it is us —

and not they — who are moving. Then there's blackness everywhere, only a narrow strip of space revealed to those of us sitting so far back of the pilot.

"Bombs away," I hear Doser say. I didn't see the robot board but he's hovering behind me now, his faux wood surface glistening much like our skin and I imagine he's been through quarantine too. Behind him is a thick door leading to the bowels of the shuttle. Neither the robot or what lies beyond that door interests me.

"Excited?" I ask Kal. He smiles again but he's anxious and I don't understand that. He should be delighted to be heading home.

"A new start to my life, I suppose," he says, his voice still subdued, eyes not quite as bright as usual, as if he is exhausted, as if he has not slept.

"You weren't in trouble, were you?" I whisper though the noise of our separation from the longhauler and the pounding as the shuttle's engines come to life are probably more than sufficient to muffle our conversation.

"In trouble? No. I am no child. But they were worried, about my intentions." He's not looking at me as he says this so I am unsure of what he makes of that, instead he's staring at the wall of the shuttle as if he sees through it.

"And what were your intentions, Kal?" I ask, realizing my slip. I've used his given name and not *Mr. Rothson* as I should have.

"Mine? Just to catch the view from the

bridge, but Decker was sure I intended to mount you." He shifts his eyes to mine, surely to see my reaction, to delight in it.

The thing about savages, I suppose, is that they are savage. I stare back in shock. There's no apology in the lines on his face.

"You might look like a woman," he says, finally, smiling again, "but you are a child. All of you are, I think."

"I am no child," I say.

He reaches across the empty seat between us and clasps my small hand. I couldn't even pull it away if I had tried, but I don't try. I am too shocked by his touch.

"Do not be offended," he says, and it is not an apology but a demand as if his just saying the words should compel me to forgive him. "Your innocence is fascinating. You have never buried a baby or watched a friend slain... never been... "

He releases my hand and stops speaking and I think he's finally found some shred of decorum. A man just doesn't speak to a woman this way. I would have walked away from him but I'm not sure I wouldn't just go drifting across the compartment and interfere somehow with the piloting.

"It is time, Kal."

I turn in my seat and realize why Kal has stopped speaking. Mr. Decker is there, using the rails above his head to keep from drifting. He's dressed smartly in a fashionable suit that would not be out of place in a corporate boardroom but seems fabricated from hardier material, like the peasant outfit I wear. There's a gun of some sort strapped to his waist, reminding me of Mr. Decker's true purpose here.

The strange door at the back of the ship is open. This is where Mr. Decker came from.

Kal nods, rising, his knees brushing mine as he exits without waiting for me to rise. I think he's going to pass me but then he leans forward, his blond hair, which has been braided into two thick strands down either shoulder, brushes my chest.

He whispers, "Stay close to your mother, child. You won't survive long in my world, without her."

I flinch, but as he walks away, with Mr. Decker, I know Kal has not said this to be cruel or nasty. He's just warning me.

CHAPTER 6

A Troubled Landing

The viewscreens painted along the sides of our shuttle erupt to life as Kal enters the back room. The screens show what he is not permitted to witness. Terrasta, in all her glory, floats before us.

Through breaks in the cloud cover I see the ice-capped southern pole and a large continent, banded by cruel badlands, lava fields, and active volcanoes to the south, with thick, dark green jungle to the north and numerous rivers quartering it. Neither of these interest me much because I won't be visiting them (and besides, I've seen vids of this all a thousand times before).

"The Moonbay!" Adira cries, pointing farther north at a bay nestled between the two primary continents; our destination.

My sister is such a geek. Like Earth, Terrasta

only has one moon but once it had two. In its distant past, the smaller moon, locked in an unstable orbit, smashed into Terrasta and created the bay and the island Adira points to now. Her excitement is peaked because the entirety of the island was created from that moon's rock and that's suppose to be cool, somehow.

This is where we will be staying for the summer, kept separate and safe from the savage clans of Terrasta until we have spread grandmother's ashes and mother completes her summer's work.

"Preparing for entry, please buckle yourselves in," the pilot says, a little later than I think he should have. Mother leans over, glancing first at Viv to her right, and then to Adira on her left, ensuring they've done as the pilot has requested. She doesn't even look over her shoulder as I tighten my strap, from shoulder to waist.

"All nice and snug, mother," I say and now she does look, not a hint of embarrassment marring her features at her having forgotten me. She tosses one of her lazy smiles at me. She's a terrible mother.

Then I remember that I've forgotten the ashes.

"Doser?" I whisper, so as not to alert the others. "Did somebody remember grandmother's urn?"

He snorts loud enough that Adira glances over at us. I shoo her away with my hand as

Doser floats conspiratorially close to my ear.

"Your mother has them," he says and I settle back into my seat. They'll be with whatever luggage mother has decided to bring. This is all in the back, with Kal.

The next several minutes are horrible, reentry nothing like the movies. The viewscreens darken, the windows in front of us fading too, covered by a protective film. Mr. Tring pilots blindly, using the gadgets on his console.

I glance at the seat Kal recently vacated with an unexpected twinge of regret. If he were sitting here, I might reach across and hold his hand, or he mine. A little human comfort in this very un-human endeavor. Now I'm alone here and he's alone back there and he's probably just as frightened, maybe more so since he knows nothing about rockets and space travel and launch windows and poorly timed reentries that result in flaming debris and quick deaths.

(And really, maybe, I don't know all that much about them, either).

Anyways, he's not here and I should be thinking of Salva and not some savage from the universe's most miserable planet. A planet without dances and online shopping and chat squads. A planet without—

I squeak as the shuttle really, *really*, vibrates as if all the vibrating before was merely a warm up to this. The temperature inside increases and sweat soaks through the clothing mother has forced us into. Scratching at it rubs the rough fibers deeper into my skin, like dragging myself across a floor of aggregate stone. But the sweating prompts the itching and it is impossible for me to resist the scratching.

I'm thrown forward, the harness straining against my chest. I scream, as my sisters do, during the final descent. It is like that first stretch of roller coaster, the giant plunge that preludes all the forthcoming dips and twists, and there's no choice but to scream. Only mother and Doser are silent.

Our screams continue as the plunge continues and continues and continues.

"Shit," I hear Mr. Tring say and that's about the last thing you want to hear from your pilot. Probably *is* the last thing passengers aboard an out of control rocket *do* hear.

We don't die and there's a brilliant flash of light as the dimmed viewscreens are restored.

"Sorry about that," Mr. Tring says, "our escort was a tad too tight; I had to make adjustments."

There are three triangular fightercraft on my side and presumably there are three others on the opposite side. The cloud cover is above us, a sprawling whorl of whites and grays and further away, darker colors, with flashes of lightning. The sun sprays across the emerald ocean waters, land a mere sliver far ahead of us. The waters are green, a contrast to the gray and blue oceans of Earth.

I ask my mother about it but Adira answers for her.

"Glaciers feed it. There are more minerals in the water, especially this close to shore."

"Which means nothing."

"Just because it's hard for you to understand, doesn't mean it is *nothing*, Miranda."

Mother adds, "Algae eats the minerals. More minerals means more algae, means more green."

I wrinkle my nose. "Disgusting." I had thought I might do some swimming but if the sea is full of algae, that's too gross. Who wants to share the water with critters?

The cabin hushes as we near land, passing first over the tip of that more isolated continent. We then cross another patch of ocean and, finally, we see the rising crags on the east coast of Landing; this is where we'll be living for the remainder of summer.

A single massive tower rises from the highest point and I'm surprised that it is so huge. Several receiver dishes cover the flat tower roof and a slash of asphalt is our runway.

The Moonbay is on the western side of this strip of land. What rock is visible beneath the thick, dark, green vegetation, is clearly different from the browns and blacks of our Earth. The rock is white, almost luminous, and I imagine in the years immediately after that doomed moon crashed here the valleys and crevasses of alabaster would have been quite the magical sight.

(Not that humans would have seen them,

the collision happened so far in the past that we hadn't yet discovered Terrasta.)

The shuttle starts banking and as our elevation decreases I spot mother's robots, swimming in the ocean.

"The cloud seeders," I say. Mother's seat creaks, as she leans over to study them better. Each seeder has a long, metal tube, a thin nose-mouth, protruding skyward. Nanos inside their swollen bladder-stomachs mix with salt water and this interaction induces them to produce chemicals. These chemicals, somehow, generate rain clouds though I'm not sure how that is possible, not until a massive seeder erupts.

"Frick!" Even Adira laughs at my outburst. A great streak of hazy white chemical spews skyward, slightly behind us, as if a volcano has exploded. If it had been any closer it would have engulfed us. "That's a hell of a sneeze."

"Not a sneeze, Miranda," Adira says, like I knew she would. "Just pumping salt and ammonium nitrate into the air."

"I *know*," I reply, more interested in the play of colors now, how the emerald water washes over the ivory shore of the island, how the sun glitters on the black, metal, seeders. The chemicals those robots spray create clouds. Storms, even. Yes, even on this hick planet, mother still controls the weather.

Another seeder erupts and then another. The pilot adjusts his angle of descent with a suddenness that bothers more than just me.

"Everything okay?" mother calls to the front

but it is Doser who replies.

"The seeders are unusually active," the robot says.

"Tell Landing to throttle them down." Which they really should have, already, I think. A moment later Doser informs us there is no reply. Without a connection through Landing the robot has no access to the satellites that control the seeders. We can't stop them.

When Adira screams I look out the window in time to see seeder spray cover a fighter. There's an orange-white flare as pieces of the ship — and of the pilot, I imagine — are tossed everywhere, some hitting us, pinging against the shuttle's hull. Even mother pales (as much as her complexion allows, anyways).

The other fighters veer to avoid the plume and their disintegrating companion.

"He's dead," I whisper.

"The satellites have returned my signal," Doser says.

"Then tell them to stop this!" I scream the command, tears rolling down my cheeks at the needless death.

"He can't," mother says, "they'll only obey instructions originating from Landing itself. A security precaution."

"Security?" Viv asks, "Nobody down there is capable of hijacking the seeders? Why worry about it?"

But mother doesn't answer that; she's pulled

her tablet into her lap instead, typing. The coast looms ahead, the tower grander than I first suspected. What I don't see is activity; the lights for the landing strip are not even flashing.

There's nothing, not a—

"There, there," I cry, frantically. "People."

They are only shadows from this far above and I don't know why I cry out, it is not as if we can speak to them. They scurry about the sheer white, cliff edges surrounding the island. We are so close to Landing now I see the lines on the landing strip. Everything will be okay; there's somebody down there to—

An alarm screeches from the front and the pilot swears again.

"What is it?" mother cries.

"Multiple incoming!" Mr. Decker says, appearing from the back, talking to the escort pilots through a black device he's carrying.

"Incoming what?" I ask. The shuttle rotates, slamming me to my right, the harness straining again, rolling away from the figures, below.

There's a banging from behind the door Mr. Decker has closed and I hear Kal's raised voice, though whether he is angry or frightened I'm not sure, the words themselves too muffled. But he's loud.

The shuttle shudders and groans and the lights, which I haven't even noticed before, flicker and die, leaving us to the shadows. Our only light comes from the cockpit.

Abruptly I'm pushed to the left and forced to grasp the empty seat. We're banking hard, now in the opposite direction, and for a brief moment, through the cockpit, I see the tower, then we are passing by it and the landing pad.

I think we're hit again because there's another grinding groan and the shriek of parted metal. The slick green of the ocean, which I had only moments before been admiring, slides into view again. We are still losing altitude, though I don't know if this is intentional anymore or if whatever has struck us has also damaged our engines. The ride down is jittery, the seats shaking violently.

The waters are a white green, capped periodically with rounded stones and they seem to me the crested humps of an impossible sea monster. Adira's Moonbay. Then this too is in our past and there's forest rushing up, the tops of trees, so many trees, more than you'd ever see on a farm on Earth.

Then I'm not seeing the trees anymore, the nose of the shuttle lifting in a final desperate act by our pilot, treetops scratching our hull.

It is inevitable. We will crash.

And right before that happens, before my head is slammed against the seat in front of me, mother whispers, "He was right."

CHAPTER 7

A Change of Plans

Salva, you wouldn't, you couldn't….

I think I woke, briefly, right after the crash and before the others pulled me free of the wreckage. I saw her. Dead. It was horrible, nothing like the vids make it seem. Her head… *sob*… smashed against the shuttle wall.

I really miss you, need you.

"Enough of that, Miranda," mother snaps and I oblige, nodding at Doser to end the message that I surely have no hope of ever sending. We are in a clearing with tall trees surrounding us and the wreckage of the still smoldering shuttle nearby. This is no natural glade: our doomed shuttle carved a trail through this forest.

(We've seen no sign of the fighters that escorted us and mother thinks they've all been shot down too. We are alone, for now.)

My forehead has been bandaged twice now and the cut seems to have stopped bleeding finally but even the pain relievers Doser has given me do nothing to stop the general tightness I feel; every muscle tender and strained. The mere weight of my head is too much for my neck. At least I have not broken my arm, like poor Adira.

And at least I'm not dead.

Viv is. (I have tried several times already not to think about that, not to think about how nasty we sisters have always been to one another.)

The pilot and Mr. Decker are dead too. Only mother and Kal appear uninjured and both busy themselves combing the wreckage for salvage. I suppose it should not surprise me that Kal does not look out of place here. This is his homeland. His shirt is now our bandages and his bare, sweat covered chest, gleams in the waning sunlight. Without him we'd all have died, suffocated by the smoke, as the shuttle immolated herself in those precious moments after impact.

It looks like most of our *stuff* survived, though not the luggage robots themselves. Mother has piled things into several piles: a pile for food, a pile for clothing, a pile for medication. There's another pile but I try to avoid looking at it.

That's where the pilot is. That's where Viv and Mr. Decker are. I don't know if it was Kal or mother who placed the two lovers side by side. If this were a story I suppose it would be a romantic gesture. Meanwhile, Doser hovers at the edge of the clearing, in a dwindling patch of sunlight. I doubt the robot has ever had to rely on his ability to convert sunlight into energy before. Like us, he's in survival mode.

Mother studies the sun for a moment and then calls to me, to help, with her chores and I start folding clothing, following mother's example. I have time to ponder where she learned to do this. Perhaps while roughing it on Terrasta in the past? Though she's never roughed it like this. Never been forced into the wilds. Still, her presence and her voice lends me strength.

The rescue patrol will come for us soon. Doser's been emitting a distress signal since the crash. Mother has promised it won't be long. They'll send more ships down, from the longhauler.

"Is she okay?" I ask, glancing at Adira, who has found her tablet. The screen is cracked but it works and my sister has lost herself again in her books.

"She'll recover," mother says and we both make a point of not glancing at Viv's corpse. We pull open each suitcase and dig through the contents. Most of it is the rough and durable clothing mother wisely brought with us but in a battered black travel sack I find grandmother's ashes.

I hand them to mother but she shakes her

head. "Put them back. You carry them." I nod, and at her direction, stuff another change of clothes into the sack. I realize she's doing the same, taking the most useful goods and cramming them into the smallest of luggage. As if packing light. As if—

"Shit!" A sudden pain sears my head from the inside. I can't move, the pain is too intense and it is followed by several aftershocks, none as potent as that initial jolt, but nevertheless debilitating.

"Doser," mother says, "she needs more."

The robot doesn't move from his sunlight, but mother guides me to him. His underside pops open, a thin arm unfolding, three chrome fingers fanning out, an injector emerging from his palm.

I don't watch as he presses it against my shoulder though I wince when I feel the needle push in. The pain dissipates almost immediately and I swoon, light-headed, mother helping me sit.

My respite is short lived. My cry has drawn Kal's attention and I notice that he's tucked Mr. Decker's brass and copper decorated revolver into his trousers.

"We need to leave," Kal says.

"I'm not fully charged," Doser protests but mother and Kal both ignore him.

"Are you sure?" she asks the savage. He nods and she turns back to the salvage pile. A moment later my sack is being shoved into my arms.

We walk the forest in silence — both because Kal has told us to keep our mouths shut and because the forest commands respect, as if chattering within its confines is a breach of etiquette. Adira is in front of me, carrying a small white satchel over her uninjured shoulder, tablet in hand, gazing often at it and still somehow avoiding the tree roots that are determined to catch my feet and send me to the moss and leaf covered ground.

Not even an hour passes before I am attacked. I can't even see my tiny assailant, I only feel fur as it brushes against my arm and despite Kal's admonition to remain silent I kind of sort of freak out. It involves rather complicated dance steps and much swatting.

"What the hell is that?" I ask as the yellow and black thing, no bigger than my thumb, flies away. Our pack of pilgrims grinds to a stop and all eyes are on me.

"A bee," Adira says, in her quiet voice, the voice I'm sure she practices every night, training herself for a future role as a curator or something.

"A what?"

"An insect, Miranda," mother adds. "It is a harmless pollinator, much needed for all these growing things."

Almost every word out of mother's mouth is unfamiliar, as if in the crash she has hit her head and learned a new language, or forgotten her old. We don't have such things back on Earth, at least not in the cities. I watch as a smaller insect lands on my hand, not far from the spot the bee vacated. It lacks the round elegance of the furrier insect, all legs and nose.

"What is this called?" I ask.

Mother manages a grim smile. "A mosquito."

Well, that's a weird word, I think, a moment before the *bastard* bites me. I swat but it escapes my wrath.

"Those," Adira says, "are not harmless."

Kal orders us to start moving again. As the insects, mostly mosquitoes, but also more bees and other critters, such as flies (which, in my opinion is the most unimaginative of names) and wasps and dragonflies, swarm around us constantly, we push our way through the claustrophobic forest. I realize now mother was more wise than cruel in her choice of our wardrobe. At least our arms and legs are covered and I am only bitten repeatedly on my neck and cheeks and hands.

The walk has changed for me, as if the bee's appearance has torn away a veil. Crashing on Terrasta has been like walking into a ballroom only to be overwhelmed by all the colors and shapes and fabrics. But gradually, as it always does at those dances, my awareness expands to accommodate the cacophony. The blur of colors becomes more distinct and I'm able to separate the trees, see them for the individuals they are, I'm also able to see the bugs the same way. Not that it makes them more acceptable but there's this wildness of color and texture and as long as the little buggers don't actually land on me, I almost admire it.

With twilight the tree shadows loom over us, the forest dark enough to be spooky, but not so dark that we cannot see our way forward. There's a rumbling noise ahead of us, growing louder, and I suspect Kal is leading us closer to it.

"Do you know where we are?" I keep my voice low. Doser is ahead of us, flying high and watching for whatever worries Kal. He strides over logs and other obstacles, setting a hurried pace.

"Not far from the ocean," he says and now I recognize the pungent odor tickling my noise. "We will follow the coast to my clan's winter camp."

"Winter?"

He gives me a strange look. I'm thinking I've offended him somehow. "Winters are hard here. When the snows arrive, my clan leaves our village in the mountains," he says. "Less snowfall and more sun on the coast."

"Will they still be there?" Adira asks; she's moved closer to us.

Kal shrugs. "Probably not; they don't linger long after the snow melts but we'll have shelter and food. We can backtrack to the village, later." Kal holds back the limbs of a tall, green leafed tree so it won't swat us. Our procession passes through and he takes up the rear. I glance back to thank him and notice pain ripple briefly across his face. Before I ask if he is okay, Adira wonders aloud, why we are hurrying.

"There's another clan, nearby," Kal says. "I fear they track us."

(Isn't that comforting?)

"Were they on the island? I saw people, below us, right before we were hit." I was not sure then, but I'm more certain now, that they carried rifles.

"I saw them too," Kal says.

"It is not possible," mother says, "*your kind* don't have such weapons. We were probably hit by a seeder, like the fighter."

The two bicker for a time about this but come to no obvious conclusions. Eventually we descend a ridge alongside the forest's edge, towards the rockier shoreline, below. I recognize a structure reaching skywards, standing proudly on the island we should have landed upon, as if taunting us.

"We call it the Tower," Kal says, "your landing place."

"Why not go there, instead?" I am unable to tear my eyes from it.

"It is forbidden," Kal says and perhaps seeing my scowl, he adds, "Besides, the waters are too deep, too vast; no man can swim them."

"What about a boat?"

"There are no boats on Terrasta!" Mother snaps.

I remember: the clans of Terrasta are denied technological advancement; any progress they make is undone swiftly.

We walk the remainder of the slope in silence but I'm unable to stop thinking about how our own society's foolishness has foiled my salvation.

Eventually the woods end and we arrive on the beach, the ocean right there, in front of us, though this is no sand-strewn slice of paradise, like on Earth, but a stretch of rough rock, covered with mangy white-feathered birds and littered with fallen trees, worn smooth by tidal pools. We make our way down towards it and mother asks Doser if there's been a reply, from Landing or the longhauler. He says there has not been.

"We'll follow the tree line tomorrow," Kal says, pointing to the east, once we reach the edge of the beach. "But, we'll have to rest here, for the night."

We set our packs down eagerly but mother and Adira don't flop down like I do. Instead they walk to the water and step in, ankle deep, as Doser roves down the beach, scouting and catching the last trickles of sunlight. Already the moon is on the horizon, swollen and unfamiliar, its face unlike the moon I've known all my life.

It will be dark soon.

Kal hisses as he leans against a fallen tree, stretching his left leg but keeping the right bent.

"You are injured." I recall his earlier pain.

"It is nothing."

"Do you want me to look at it?" I ask.

"And what would you do?" he says, his voice and eyes hard enough that I avert my gaze, directing my eyes instead to the ground. It is full of crawling horrors I hadn't noticed before but even their presence is insufficient to dismiss the insulting tone of Kal's words. He is such a contradiction; one moment kind, the next cruel.

"I don't know. Maybe clean it or something."

"Or something," he says, "that is your people's way. I've heard it so many times before, this and your other vague words. You don't know how to tend a wound or to make your own shelter or clothing or even cook a meal."

I wish I might have protested but nothing he said was inaccurate. Still I pout; I want to help but don't know how. We are utterly reliant on an injured man who does not respect us. What are his intentions? Landing is right there, in front of us, and he wants to lead us away. He must see my worry because he suddenly smiles.

"No worries, Miranda," he says, "I spoke harsh, I am unused to being around such inadequate women."

"That's your apology?"

He shrugs and I move away, down the beach, and pull out my phone. Of course it can't make a call but at least it has my music on it.

I've just started listening to booming pop lyrics, a mix of automated, random music bound together with the jamming excitement of Squishsocks when mother and Adira undress. I pull my earbuds free and stuff them and the phone back into my pant pockets as I rush towards the water.

A white splash of moonlight washes over us and the bay and I gasp as an illumination appears beneath the waters. It is the moon rock itself and it is brilliant, almost blinding. My mother and sister are dark shadows flickering across the illuminated seafloor.

"He's watching you," I say. They wash themselves, ignoring my words.

"Who cares?" mother says with a deep, rare, uneven, laugh, "what does it matter? Here?" There's a quality to her voice that unnerves me; she's always been as solid as the rock she stands upon.

"How can you be so stubborn?" I lower my voice. "We shouldn't be giving him any ideas. We are at his mercy."

"Mercy?" Mother glares at me. "There is no mercy here; don't expect it, don't hope for it."

Adira, standing behind mother and up to her neck in the water, pales.

"Don't say that," I protest, "we'll be rescued. We'll go home and everything will return to normal—"

"Shut up!" Adira cries, her normally placid face contorted in rage. "There is no normal, not anymore. Viv is dead and all you care about is going back to Earth, to your stupid and vapid friends, and your pointless balls."

Mother's hand snakes out, clasping Adira's and both of them start crying, their tears reflecting moonlight. *My mother is crying.* It is then that I realize what they are doing. They are not bathing for the sheer perversity of it, to tease Kal.

When Viv hit her head and it exploded, her blood must have covered them. This is what they wash away now.

The water rolls in, lapping at my ankles and it is so cold, I step back. The cold is a shock, a slap, though of an entirely different sort than my sudden realization. I've needed to pee since I woke. But the bathroom on the shuttle had been a crushed heap of metal and plastic and then we were fleeing and now… now the urge is irresistible.

"I have to… go…." With those words I'm back to being a little girl trailing after Viv, clutching her outstretched hand as we rush up and down the stairs of our apartment, chasing after a plaything robot.

"So did I." It takes me a second to figure out that Adira means she's peed in the water. I retreat, back to shore.

"That's gross!"

Mother snaps, "Damn it, Merry. Find a log or something… enough with your silliness."

CHAPTER 8

A Savage Attack

By the next morning I'm an expert (if not a fan) of relieving myself in the woods.

After twenty minutes of searching last night I found the perfect log and today I only need five to kick and shoo it free of bugs. I drop my trousers and settle onto the bark, blocking thoughts of the wild creatures of Terrasta worming their way into my privates.

I haven't slept well but it's not just the crash, it's what mother said to me, last night. *Your silliness.* She has no respect for me and I know that here, given our circumstances, that ought be the least of my concerns but it chafes me, her lack of patience with my lack of ability. What had she expected?

We've been shot down! Attacked! Things like this don't happen on Earth. Mother, Viv, maybe even Adira, are all better suited than I for surviving here, because they at least have entertained the possibility of such things happening. They realize Terrasta has enemies. But nobody hates me; I'm nobody's enemy.

I'm a Terrastan, daughter of Drea. Impossible to consider that our family is mortal, let alone the target of any attack. With our resources there is not a person, not a company, not even a nation, that wouldn't be subject to the worst possible retribution. Mother controls the world's food supply. You do not go up against that. Really, there's no messing with us. At all.

I'm interrupted from my thoughts (just as I'm buckling my pants) by a scream and I rush through the forest bordering the beach, back to camp, stumbling over loose rocks and slippery moss. There's shouting now and I hear Kal. A thin column of smoke rises and maybe he has started a fire, I think. After all, he's a savage, he'd know how to do something like that. Maybe Adira burned herself on it. Just a burn.

I'm rationalizing, I know, but I have to. Our attackers could not have tracked us. It is impossible. Yet I'm wrong again, so very wrong.

I stop in the woods, more by instinct than any actual wisdom on my part.

Several men surround Kal, all bare chested and with the same long, almost-white hair as he. The revolver is on the ground and he's brandishing a half meter of pipe that he salvaged from the crash. Kal swings it weakly; there's blood flowing down his chest and an angry gash across his head.

Mother's not there. Nor is Doser. Just these savages and Kal and....

(Are these the men who shot down our shuttle? They carry no rifles, no stunsticks, no launchers; just bows, arrows, and spears, which I've only ever seen in the toy sets that Marcus collected as a kid.)

I almost cry, but shove my hand into my mouth to stop myself. Adira's face down in the sand, between me and the men, and she's on fire. There's a flaming arrow through the middle of her back, and mother's practical clothing is not so practical as to be fireproof. There's other arrows too, in the sand, wisps of black smoke rising from them.

My little sister is dead.

I want to help Kal against his attackers and (maybe) if the man nearest him hadn't swung hard with a solid wedge of polished wood, a club covered with thick yellow-orange spikes, I might have. But that swing knocks Kal to his knees, a cloud of loose rock flying up from his impact. The man behind him kicks him square in the back and he's face forward and then they are all climbing on him. I should be able to understand them but their voices are thick, guttural, and deep; their words incomprehensible.

But I hear Kal's name spoken, they know him. Are they from his clan? Or are they from that other clan, and if so, how would they know him? It makes no sense.

From the corner of my eye I see movement, new movement, and I have to bite down harder on my knuckles now, to keep my mouth shut because Adira raises her head and stares at me. She's not dead.

I'm watching them both, Adira-not-dead, and Kal. Flicking my gaze from one to the other. I'm trembling 'cause I'm scared. There's no dodging that. There's tears streaming down my eyes and only some sort of common sense that I'm sure mother doesn't think I have keeps me from crying out and flailing useless fists against those men. All the while I'm smelling smoke and burning flesh (and there's no way to describe how horrible that smells).

Where is mother? When will she come sweeping in to save us?

Maybe she's already dead.

"Impossible," I whisper. Adira raises her head again and I want to warn her not to make any noise so I stare at her, I really stare. Her eyes meet mine, I'm sure of it, though I'm almost fully buried inside the mass of trees and shrubs and prickly things around me.

She knows I'm there.

The men are busy beating Kal, four of them throwing blows with their fists, three others, standing off to the side. Two are father and son, I think, judging by how similar their faces are. Both have long faces and neatly trimmed beards peaking at the apex of their chins, though the elder's beard is gray, the younger, brown. The older man is wrinkled too, something I've never seen before. He's an actual old person. He's Ancient and his eyes are terrible and empty pools of malevolence.

The younger man is more frightening. Every once in a while he kicks Kal and laughs and when he does it is a wicked sound. He's the truest Savage.

Nobody notices Adira or me. We're not especially close, as sisters, but I'll never forget that kindness of hers, she telling me about Viv and Salva's past. That unprovoked act of kindness. But it doesn't matter if she's my sister: when somebody's burning alive, you have to save them, right? It is the only civil thing to do when there are no robots or adults or heroes around.

I think I might skirt around the edge of the bush and drag her into the shrubs with me. Hide her. Mother's not dead, that's impossible. We hide, she finds us, we find a way to Landing and back to Earth. It is all in the range of possibilities. All of it.

Except I don't move.

I stare at Adira. She's trembling, my sister no longer burning, merely smoldering. And yes, she's seeing me through her dirty, tear streaked face. She starts to move her arm, as if to prop herself into a crawl. All I have to do is the same, a movement, a catalyst towards action.

Except I can't. I want to, I know I need to, but I'm too frightened. With all my will I try to move my fingers from where they've taken a death hold on a slender shaft of a tree, the bark digging into the skin of my palm. My fingers twitch, a brief movement, enough, that I fight through my stupor—

And then Kal is shrieking, a sound I never imagined he might make. My head pivots to him, to the two cruel men sneering down at him and a third man, who's not actively engaged in hurting Kal. He is neither as young as the younger or as old as the older but he stands behind them, his head averted, as if in disagreement over the violence. I think he tells them to stop and there's a short argument but he finally shakes his head, walks away.

Through the gaps between his attacker's arms and legs I catch snatches of Kal's final moments. A man stands on Kal's back, Kal's hair in his hand, tilting Kal's head up. Others are on his arms and legs. And the last takes an awful blade and begins to cut, to saw.

I clamp my eyes shut but my ears still tell me the story. They decapitate Kal slowly and somebody, somewhere needs to stop this but when his crying, screaming, begging, ends, I know it hasn't happened. I know that they have finished. Finished with Kal.

He wasn't suppose to die; he belongs here. He is a survivor. I'm not sure if I'll ever forget those few minutes alone on the bridge, me seeing, if briefly, that playful side of him, that gentle side. He was a savage but he was a good man, I'm sure of it. He didn't deserve this.

Adira screams and I open my eyes. She's crawled, towards the bush, during Kal's painful end, but the savages have seen her and realized she is not dead.

I can't watch this. I can't watch them kill her. A braver sister might have fought them off but not me. They drag Adira to her feet and she shrieks in pain when they toss her from man to man and I'm not sure their intent but I don't think they want to kill her. They man handle her instead and I see that she still has her tablet clasped to her and the Savage tears it from her, crushing it beneath his leather-wrapped feet.

They're all laughing and she's crying and it is not right, not right at all, their taking pleasure in her suffering but then I realize what they are doing, that her back is to the third man, the man who argued earlier with the other two and he's reaching for Adira. There's a *snap* and he breaks the arrow shaft protruding from her back.

My little sister collapses but is caught and lifted over the broad shoulders of the Savage, and then, after a few moments of scavenge, they taking our bags of food and clothing and the revolver, leaving me only with my small satchel (which holds little more than grandmother's ashes) they leave.

They take Adira.

They won't hurt her; she's worth too much. They'll ask for a ransom and when that is paid and Adira brought back, mother's vengeance, shall be a terrible thing. (But the part of me that worries thinks ransom is the furthest thing from such savage minds as these.)

The Savage, with Adira still over his shoulder, pauses to lift Kal's head by the hair, swinging it like a child swings a pail of sand. He takes it and they disappear into the woods. The beach is quiet now except for the occasional squawk of the white and black birds waiting to dart in and claim what the savages have left.

Still, I cannot move.

I'm crying and sucking in my breath so my sobs are inaudible and I'm rocking myself, hands around my knees. Eventually it starts to rain but I don't move at all. This is not right, this is so much worse than I ever imagined possible. It is beyond comprehension, my mind almost shattering and I'm not sure if I sat there for minutes or hours before a firm hand lands on my shoulder.

Then... finally... I scream.

CHAPTER 9

The Man Who Was Right

Mother slaps me across the cheek.

"Get your ass moving." Her grip moves from my shoulder to my triceps, dragging me away. Her face is paler than I ever imagined possible and seeing that makes me finally act. We stumble from the bush and walk past the campsite without stopping. I can't help glancing at Kal's headless body and for the rest of my life I'll wish I hadn't.

"Adira?" I ask once we are past the carnage. I slip often on the rain slick rocks but mother is more graceful. Yet now my question makes her stumble. She swipes at her hair, pushing damp strands from her eyes; though her hair is shorter than mine it is still waterlogged.

"We can't go after her, on our own. They carried her to the north, maybe northwest."

And we were heading east. "We can't abandon her to them."

"And what might we do, Merry? How might *we* rescue her?"

"I—"

"I *want* to go after her too," mother says and her voice is on the verge of cracking. "You have no idea. No idea what it is to be a mother, unable to protect her children."

I can't respond to that, though as we walk the next few hours, in more or less silence, I'm thinking about how I might have been able to save my little sister and how I wasn't brave enough to do so. For a long time I'm alone in my head, on the beach, weighed down by my guilt but eventually my stomach grumbles loud enough that mother hears it.

"I left my backpack with Doser. It has food and water," mother says.

"I don't understand how you knew we would be attacked."

"I didn't. Kal and I… we disagreed after you left. I walked down the beach with Doser and then sent him east, to scout the way to Landing."

"Can Doser protect us, from them?" I ask.

"Does he have weapons, you mean?"

"Yeah, I guess."

Mother snorts. "He's built for drug delivery, not warfare. He'll be of no help to us, except as a scout, I suppose. You've watched too many of

92

your brother's scify programs."

The way she says *your brother*, it's full of… distaste. I know the two of them have an even stranger relationship than she and I but I don't know why, other than that old and often trotted out platitude that mother never wanted a son.

"Do you even like Marcus?"

She snorts again. "I'm obligated to love him. And it is not his fault, that he's a mistake, right?"

I'm not sure if she's addressing the rhetorical question to me or herself or to fate, in general.

"I understand you *think* he's a mistake," I say, though I don't know how, with all our influence, a mistake like that could have happened, "but why didn't you want a son?"

"I dislike males, is all. We don't need to talk about it."

Mother is lying and not doing a good job of disguising it. "That's a crap answer, mother, and you know it."

"Merry, Merry, Merry," she mocks, like she used to when I was younger. "The thing is, that there is something wrong with Terrastan men. My brother, my father, they were flawed."

"You are kidding."

"No. I'm not. Bastards all died long before you were born."

Died. I don't like the way she says that and I don't like the way her eyes travel and gaze far away, as if to avoid seeing what is close to her.

"What did they—"

"*That* is not important. But let's just say that

trace of evil, I had hoped to extinguish."

"If there's a better man than Marcus, I've never met him."

"Perhaps," she allows and that is all, though this I'll definitely talk to her about after we are safe. After we rescue Adira.

Even with my feet growing weary and sore and blistery after days of marching, that's the thought that is primarily in my mind. That I need to make up for my failure earlier. I don't know how we'll do it. But mother, she'll figure it out. She always does.

I'm not sure my mother is telling me the truth, or at least not the entire truth. She insists she did not know about the impending attack on our camp, but I'm remembering something else now. Maybe it is the long walk down the dreary, gray beach, and the nose-hair curling stench of the ocean, that is reminding me of those last few moments before the shuttle crashed, or maybe it is the long silence between us.

"Mother, you said 'he was right', earlier, after we were shot."

"I did?" Her voice is guarded and reserved again, as if she's tired of me pestering her with questions. Or tired of supplying answers, as if she needs all her secrets, as if talking about them diminishes them.

"Yes. You did."

"What does it matter now?"

"It matters, mother."

She sighs and I think she's not going to answer me, until she does. "I... I knew we'd lost contact with Landing. Knew it months ago."

"What!?"

"Oh, do calm down, Merry. Landing goes offline every few years. Not a big deal. It's just that this time it coincided with our arrival. Your Mr. Durand, he's the one who warned me. He wanted me to wait till he was ready to send a properly equipped expedition with us. I thought... well, what I thought doesn't matter, now. He was worrying too much."

Was this why we had a fighter escort? Had Salva anticipated we might have troubles? "And you," I say, "were not worried enough."

She doesn't argue that because she can't and she knows it. This isn't right or fair. Why didn't Salva warn me? Sure, he'd asked me to stay but he didn't explain why. I would've, if I'd known. I would've insisted on it. I would have saved Viv and Adira.

But it's mother I'm most angry with; she's endangered us by keeping secrets. Her head is always buried so deep in her research that she's unable to consider the larger picture.

I struggle to fit the pieces together.

"You said you sent Doser ahead, *before* the attack. Were you not going to follow Kal?"

Mother stops, slipping her hand into her black vest for a flask of water. She hands it to me and I sip the water, wondering why she hadn't offered it to me earlier. I've never been thirsty before and I'm unable to stop myself from gulping it down.

"I don't know," she admits and I'm floored. Mother always knows. "Trust is a precious commodity. I did not want to be at the mercy of his clan. And I know a secret he did not."

"A secret?"

"There's another way to Landing."

All my life I've been taught that Terrasta is a pool, teeming with a diversity of life. Yes, it is primitive and lacking our sophistication, but also, in its innocence, it is insurance against humankind's tendency to destroy even as we create. A backup plan, a savegame.

This planet is our promised salvation in case of misfortune. In videos and lectures it is always portrayed with soft tones and long sunsets and beautiful and vivid shots of airborne birds or dolphins frolicking or herds of antelope running free. The clans may live a hard life but it is a life without the wearying complications and responsibilities of civilization.

It is paradise.

But if paradise is decapitations and abductions, parched throats and empty stomachs, foot blisters and rain soaked clothing, then paradise can go and suck the big one.

We walk. And we walk. (And oh, did I mention, we walk?)

Mother talks when prompted but it is no

longer I doing the prompting. I'm angry with her (and, maybe, I've also ran out of questions). She is prompted instead by what we discover. A clutch of red and blue flowers, for example, draws her attention, and she tells me their names and genetic lineages. I learn that the nearby trees are birch and poplar. That farther north I will find pine — those that resemble the robotic trees that self-assemble themselves every Christmas — and firs and cedar.

Now we've stopped and there's a cluster of thick bushes growing at the base of a birch tree. She's showing me the tiny, round, blue flowers on the bush.

"Berries," mother says. We've both given up shielding ourselves from the rain, which at best is a light drizzle, and at worst, when the wind picks up, is a cold razor blade against our exposed skin. When I kneel it is into soft, muddy, soil.

Mother slides the fruit into her mouth, smiling, and when she offers me one I take it, biting into it gingerly instead of popping it into my mouth. Juice sprays onto my chin and when I wipe it away my hand is covered with the blue fluid. It is sweet. Somebody has added too much sugar.

Mother picks more and though the taste takes some getting used to, I'm ravenous and I devour them. After a few more minutes of quiet forage, mother frowns, pulling a cluster of reedy plants growing alongside the berries free, exposing their roots.

"Are these edible?" I ask, never in my life imagining I'd consider chowing down on weeds grown in actual dirt. Tiny insects scurry away and I reconsider.

"If you boiled them, yes." She flakes dirt from the roots. "But these are flawed."

"Oh." Really what else is there to say when your mother is more concerned about a stupid plant than her kidnapped daughter? She's turning the earth over with her hand.

"This is wrong. Very wrong." She grabs a squirming, tubular creature, about as long as my finger.

"What is that?"

She gives me a curious look. "A worm, Merry. Nothing to be terrified of. These creatures are good for the soil, back on Earth."

"Then what's wrong?"

"It shouldn't be here. We did not bring worms to Terrasta." She discards the critter and tears apart the plant, examining its insides. "Jesus Christ. These are not even my crops, my seed."

"How do you know?"

"I know." She tosses it all to the ground and orders me to pick some more berries, and then we set off again. We make slower progress because mother insists on stopping often, picking plants, examining them, sometimes even sliding leaves or roots into her pockets (which, really, isn't going to smell nice in a day or two).

Still, it won't take us that long before we are safe, I remind myself. Mother has told me her secret way to Landing.

Ahead, at a narrow point, between Landing's island and this shore we follow, there's a console, hidden in a cave in the rock. Activate it and a bridge will emerge, from the bay. Mother explains that it was for hauling seed and other materials, back in the early days, when the planet was first being developed.

Our path is becoming more unwelcoming, the round, awkward rocks are now sheets of flat, black stone, with tidal pools left behind when the tides withdraw. Red squirming things crawl between the pools and I try to stay as close to the forest boundary as I dare but that too becomes more unpleasant with each kilometer.

The trees are thicker and taller here, a hill between us and the forest rising, with more of that black, angular rock jutting up, forming a partial wall, as if the woods have fortified themselves against the ocean. And for good reason. The water pounds the shore, aggressive, white-capped waves smashing the rock wall. To enter the water we'd have to jump from the growing cliffs we are now ascending. This is no longer a beach, but instead a sprawl of rough and cruel crags.

It is mother that sees the starship first. This is not surprising considering that I'm more or less studying my feet as the beach has become repetitious: the same dull rock, the same thundering waves. She points and rushes ahead (and where she finds this extra energy, I can't say). I plod behind her, even when I realize what she's discovered. No point in rushing towards it. There's not much left.

It did not land *here*. The central tube of the escort fighter is still intact and if it had hit the rock directly, I don't think it would still be in one piece. Not that it is functional, in the least, for it is missing both wings and the rear section and the cockpit itself has been torn open.

The pilot is gone.

Mother clambers up the side of it, peering in, even pressing buttons but there's no chance the comm's going to work. The fighter must have crashed into the sea and been washed ashore.

"What are these?" I ask, showing mother several rents in the steel hull, long, angular slashes beside the cockpit. She leaps off, eyes wide, briefly staring out to sea, before turning.

"There." I follow her pointed finger. It's hard to say but I think I see what she sees; a trail through the litter of dead plants and gnarled wood that is everywhere on this planet (not even an army of robots could get this place clean and tidy). A large creature recently moved through here.

"It took the pilot," mother says.

"It?"

"The fool, the bloody, damned, crazy, fool."

Goosebumps spring to life, as if I've heard the most awesome new song of the week. But these are not good bumps. These are something else.

100

"We never should have let them come here."

"What are you talking about, mother!" I am dreadfully close to panic. Her conversations are one-sided, as if I'm not a worthy participant, but merely a sounding board for her mutterings. I'm tired of being half in the dark.

Or maybe I'm just tired because when she doesn't answer me I grab her by the shoulder. She glances at me and shrugs free from my grip.

"Durand's a fool," she says.

"Salva?"

She shakes her head. "His father, his family. They… wanted to create new life. To improve *the human condition*; their words, not mine."

I shudder but decide now is not the time to mention that Salva might possibly be following in his family's footsteps.

"Did you know Salva's dad?"

"Yes, of course," she snaps, "and this proves he did what he said he wouldn't. That he did what mother always worried he might." It takes me a blink or two to clue in. She's talking about *grandmother*.

"Something Gehum *created*, took the pilot?"

"It appears, Merry, that there's worse here, than savages. There's monsters too."

The clouds break for a few hours in the afternoon, but there's no pleasure in that warm, angry sun above us. Our exposed skin grows hot and soon I'm cursing that roiling ball of fire above us. It is a mercy when the gray clouds roll in again, shading us from the rain.

"There." Mother points to an unnatural path leading into the hills and the forest. Away from the beach. I shudder at the thought of entering those woods. "We have no choice, the beach ends, Merry, you see that it does. We have to climb now before we can't."

She says the words as if speaking at a press conference or to a simpleton and if I had any more energy or any fuller of a stomach or any less parched lips, I'd have argued her condescension. Instead I clamber up the incline behind her. She has made it clear that of the three daughters that accompanied her to Terrasta, I'm the least she wants along, now. And really, is she wrong? I don't have Adira's knowledge or Viv's strength, or my mother's coordination, it seems. Twice I stumble and am forced to crawl on hands and knees, like an animal, cutting my palms and fingers on the sharp rock.

The rain has coated everything, making what ought to have been an awkward uphill walk a sloughing, messy, climb, instead. Beyond my sight, I know those bastard seeders are spraying their chemicals into the air, triggering more rainfall after blasted rainfall. And sure enough, before we finish our climb it starts raining again.

Terrasta used to be a dry planet, unable to support the range of life it now does. With the seeders and the emergence of an actual weather system (a weather system my grandmother supposedly built) the planet became capable of sustaining Earth-based lifeforms. But if everything rots, if everything is wet all the time, what kind of life is there for this planet's inhabitants?

"Mother," I ask, after we've reached the halfway point in our climb. "These monsters, are you sure they are from Gehum?"

She glances at me. "What do you mean?"

I'm somewhat reassured to hear exhaustion in her own voice; it means I'm not entirely deficient.

"There was native life here, before," I say. "Could it have—"

"Jesus Christ," she snaps, "don't you ever study? Ever read?"

I flush, pausing in my exertions to accept another lecture from the bitch. When she's finished, she tries explaining.

"It wasn't like there were creatures running about here, Merry. Just microscopic organisms living in the seas."

"What if they evolved?" I say, not caring that this will launch another exasperated sigh and another lecture. I'm enjoying the brief rest; my thighs and shins hurt and my gut is oddly tight.

"Single cell organisms evolving into monsters, larger than you or I, in fewer than the handful of generations we've occupied this planet? Seriously, Merry, what is wrong with you? It takes generation after generation for evolution to create new species. Millions of years before we'd see change like that."

I shut up. Her voice is becoming louder and

if there are monsters in the woods, Terran or Terrastan, I don't want them alerted to my indignant mother. Even if I do kind of want to see her swallowed up (if only to silence her).

When we reach the top of the hill, I suck in a deep breath, the ocean air strong and full of the stench of dead sea life and salt. My stomach recoils, though the smell is no stronger than before; I realize it is the exertion, the effort, I've put into the uphill march, and maybe the thought of headless Kal and my burning sister, and the initial effects of withdrawal (I've missed several doses now of the concoctions civilized people use to keep sane and healthy).

All of it together, is overwhelming. I double over, vomiting up the berries. I kneel and gag as light-blue fluid splashes the moss below me.

Mother waits a few moments and then asks "Are you ready, Merry, to proceed?"

I wipe my mouth with the back of my arm, the fabric scratching my face.

"Yes, mother."

CHAPTER 10

A River Crossing

We meet up with Doser just after Terrasta's feeble moon rises. Last night I was too exhausted to even glance at the night sky but now I realize that the moon is indeed smaller than Earth's, and obviously so. The constellations are all the brighter for it but they offer no comfort either because I do not recognize them.

The ocean is almost deafening, battering the shore with fury and we don't hear the whirl of Doser's motors as he drifts through the woods beside us, until he's in front of us, seemingly conjured by the shadow clutched branches of the wizened trees.

"Good evening!"

It takes all my will not to throw a stone at him, to silence his unnatural exuberance. Well, not really; I hardly have the energy to bend and retrieve a stone, let alone throw it. I collapse, on the damp earth, no more than an arm's length away from the edge of what is now a sheer cliff-face, overlooking the jagged shoreline below. The wind howls and plucks at my long hair but I barely notice.

"Jerk." If my words offend Doser, he does not show it.

Mother urges us into the tree line, suggesting we set up camp for the night. I do not protest though it means having to stand again. We settle in and Doser tells us that ahead there is a large crevasse worn through the rock where a river drains into the sea. Our path is blocked.

"Is there a way past it?" Mother asks, unhooking the satchel he's been carrying for us.

"I scouted several kilometers to the north but found no better route. That does not mean there is not one, farther upriver." He pauses a moment, looking around.

"Where are the others?"

Mother doesn't answer, she digs instead through the satchel and tosses me a granola bar. Between bites I bring Doser up to speed. Mother hands me a water bottle and taking sips of that allows me to pace my eating.

"The savage is dead?"

I nod.

"And Adira's been taken?"

We both nod.

I don't think the robot's programming is up to the challenge of dealing with such dreadful news and he says nothing more as mother and I eat our rations. I glance skywards, scanning the stars for a familiar object, the longhauler.

"It is gone," mother's voice intrudes on my search.

"They wouldn't abandon us!" The whole point in getting to Landing is to communicate with the starship and have them pick us up. Now, even once we get there, we'll have to wait for another ship.

"Miranda is right," Doser says, "no reason for them to have left orbit."

Mother makes no reply, she is in fact so silent that the robot repeats himself and my mother wrings her hands together, bites her lip.

"The thing is," she says, finally, "I think somebody at Gehum ordered them to leave."

"Salva?" It is impossible.

"He was not pleased with… a recent decision I made."

"A decision? What sort of decision, mother?"

"We ended Kal's term two years early. Kal was to be the last."

No more Promoted? "But, why?"

"Because I've terminated Gehum's involvement with Terrasta. Their contract ended and I did not renew it. Your grandmother and I, we had decided this, before her death."

"Salva wouldn't do that, wouldn't abandon me—"

"He would not have known we would crash. He would have simply assumed we'd be stranded at Landing for a few extra months, until I sent for another longhauler. He would have just been making a point, to me. Hell, maybe it wasn't him. Gehum is a sprawling company and he's still familiarizing himself with it. There are likely entire divisions he does not know about." Mother takes a breath before continuing, "Regardless, their attempts here have gone too far. And now that I've seen evidence of their monsters and the violence the clans inflict upon each another, I know we made the right decision. Gehum is breeding savagery."

"The brain scans," Doser says.

"What scans?" I interrupt, not wanting them to fall into a conversation I am only a mere witness to.

Mother answers, "Evolution acts over millions of years, but in the brain scans we obtained from the last few Promoted, we discovered a faster rate of *change* than is natural. Their brains are growing larger."

"Gehum is making them smarter?"

"No," mother says with a tight smile, "larger doesn't mean smarter. Their brains are losing their sophistication, becoming simpler. Devolving."

"That's not possible."

"It is. The savages are transitioning into a primitive state. Gehum is intentionally making them more… wild."

Why would they want them to be more savage? "Maybe it is about the diversity," I offer. "The more different they become, from us, the more… variance they give our own genes, right? Isn't this what you always talk about? That a monoculture is bad, susceptible to a targeted disease. That only diversity guarantees longterm success?"

"You have learned some of your lessons, Merry, *and* this is why we've built the pool, to preserve agricultural diversity. But there's a point where two streams of genes become too different to produce offspring. They become separate species."

I remember how I responded after Kal touched me and I cringe. "They are not… the same as us, anymore?"

"Not yet. I believe there are still enough similarities, but if the rate of change continues, at this pace they will no longer be our kind of human. We had to stop Gehum from continuing this work."

Gehum breeding monsters? Some legacy of my love's vile father, surely. A rogue faction, rotting away inside Salva's company. When we reach Landing I will warn him and he will set this right.

I can't help him until we are safe and the sooner I sleep, the sooner I'll wake. The sooner I'll reach Landing. I ask Doser for a shot and he obliges, though warns that he's running low on the chemicals he needs to compose our drugs. Another reason to reach Landing, soon.

The chemical mixture sends me to a swift slumber, with barely enough time for me to worry about what will happen to us tomorrow.

I wake before the others. Crawling things have taken advantage of me throughout the night and now, with the first blush of sunlight, I brush several multi legged critters from my wet hair with my fingers. I flinch, my work half done, when a tremor shakes the forest. I turn my head slowly because there's a sudden stillness, all the animal sounds I'm becoming accustomed to, now absent; only the persistent tap-tap of falling rain.

Doser hums contently, in a state of hibernation, maximizing his charging throughput. Mother is still asleep and, relaxed, I see both Viv and Adira in her features. Traces of my sisters, one dead, one… one suffering an unimaginable fate. I'm with the woman who gave birth to me and I feel more alone than I ever have, in all my life.

I stare back at the forest. The trees are more than silent watchers, I'm sure the whispering of their leaves incites the wild beasts. We have no fire. We have no weapons. We are helpless. This is what the trees say. The message they pass on to Gehum's monsters.

"Enough," I whisper, silencing my imagination. I rise and stretch my arms, my back cracking. There's no reason to think that a monster prowls outside the radius of our camp. No reason at all, except that when a fallen branch snaps, a loud, retort, an echo that almost makes me wet myself, I *know*.

"Mother!" I punctuate my outburst with a boot to her ribs. She wakes and I rush towards Doser, hissing at him to reboot. There's a nerve wracking whirling sound as his systems come online. How long does it take, I think, for his operating system to load? If I were Adira I'd have known the answer, right down to the number of seconds.

I watch the woods and count. One. Two. Three.

Forty-seven.

It takes forty seven seconds for Doser to wake, for his eye diode to ignite, for the retracted solar panels to fold inside him and his mahogany shell to snap closed. Mother's on her feet before then and I whisper a warning to her. Two pinpricks of light are glowing in the woods; two yellow eyes are staring at us.

Doser drifts towards the hidden monster, his retractable claw dangling below him like kite string. I'm not sure what I'm expecting him to do. He has no weapon; mother has already said this. But maybe in the stew of hallucinogens and pain killers carried inside him there's a chemical capable of subduing the beast. Or perhaps he has a sonic whistle, capable of stunning an enemy, or even—

Doser dips low to the ground and the tines of his claw close over a stone.

"Go on! Get out of here!" It is not the robot's voice I hear, but Kal's, a dead man's echo. Doser throws the rock at the beast and though robots can't throw worth a damn, there's a sharp yelp. I jump, heart thudding, as whatever is there, scurries away, the undergrowth rustling in its passage.

"What was it?" I ask, as Doser floats back into view, retracting his arm.

The robot chirps. "Not even a thank you, for my bravery? My heroics."

Mother actually laughs but I'm not fond of humoring robots. They are not people and etiquette is unnecessary when dealing with them. That is entirely the point of their existence; a subset of society wherein we can be ourselves, wherein there are no facades.

I ask my question again.

"Didn't see it," Doser says.

"A wolf, maybe?" mother asks. A wolf is like a dog, I remember, and dog's were not so terribly fearsome. A few of my friends even own the irritating poop and noise machines; though most prefer synthetic facsimiles.

(I didn't own either. Not the nurturing type.)

Doser snorts. "No, it was too tall. The eyes were almost two meters from the ground"

"Only one?"

"No, it had two eyes," Doser says.

Mother rolls her own eyes at the robot's quip. "Was there only one *creature*?"

Doser beeps in confirmation but we still pack quickly, just in case. Fifteen minutes later we are walking again, every step painful, my blister covered feet merciless. Twice I let Doser stick his needle in me, to numb the pain.

Well before noon, we reach the tumultuous river that cuts her path through solid rock. This is trail's end, as far east as we can travel without crossing. To the south is a sprawl of black rock leading to the sea, almost barren of life, except for a few hardy weeds surviving in shallow depressions of wind filled soil. To our north, the forest stretches, rising in slow increments until in the far off distance it towers over us as we now tower over the coast. From where I stand I take in the sweeping vistas of the Moonbay and the massive, ivory crags of the island. Landing's gleaming black, tower, rises above it all.

The river rushes forward, thick and frothy and pushing hard past the few boulders cresting its surface. These large rocks were brought downstream by this unstoppable force of nature in some unknowable past. Doser tells us that it is ten meters across. Which, really, isn't that far when you think about it. Except that perhaps half a kilometer south, there is a waterfall leading to a lower branch of the river. The twisting outflow below that leads into the sea. We hardly hear ourselves over the boom and clash of the waterfall.

"How much weight can you carry?" mother shouts above the din. The robot hums in surprise.

"If you are suggesting that I carry you across," Doser says, "you either overestimate my abilities or severely underestimate your girth."

Mother seems to ignore the wisecrack but if it weren't a matter of life or death that we keep Doser around I'd have deactivated the son of a bitch and punted him into the river. Nothing wrong with my girth.

"The only obvious choice," Doser says, "is for me to scout ahead and you two follow." He orients himself north. Towards the creepy-ass forest.

I haul my satchel over my shoulder. We hardly have any food; the satchel is too light, but my shoulders, underneath my tunic, are sore from where the strap has dug into the flesh. I suspect, on Terrasta, I'm always going to be sore.

"But you've already scouted that way," mother says. "How far, again?"

"Six hours."

"Six hours," she repeats, "and you found no safer crossing?"

"No," Doser admits. "But surely the river narrows, somewhere up north. When I find a crossing, I'll backtrack and bring you to it."

"Sure." I start forward but mother stops me.

"No. We cross here." She sets her satchel down and points at the rocks peeking out of the water. "From there, to there, to there."

"That's hardly advisable," Doser says and I nod in vigorous agreement. Mother's not thinking straight, grieving over Big Sister, worried over Little Sister. The water moves too fast, she'd never reach the first rock before being swept towards the waterfall.

114

But mother never listens. She rolls her boots and socks off and dips her blistered feet into the water, wincing.

"That's frigid."

"This isn't going to work," I say. "Even if you cross, I can't."

"You and the robot go around then," she says, turning on us both. "But I will not waste hours, maybe days, finding another crossing point."

"Mother… we have enough food, if we skimp, to last us a day or two. We have the time."

"We *might* have the time," she snaps, "but Adira, she doesn't. Or have you forgotten?"

No. I haven't forgotten. I'll never give myself permission to forget.

"Then send me ahead," Doser says, "you two search for a safer crossing and I'll fly over the bay, to Landing."

"We've already talked about that, robot," mother says, her voice betraying her worry, her irritability. "Leave it alone."

Then without further word, she steps into the river. I tense, expecting her to be swept away, immediately but though the water is swift, my mother is a goddess. She walks with tentative but certain strides, ensuring solid footing before advancing.

It takes several nervous minutes but she reaches the first rock and circles around it. The water hasn't quite reached her waist, but as she steps away from the first rock she seems to be struggling more against the flow.

When she reaches the second rock I release the breath I've been holding. My mother, my crazy, mother, who has always lived her life in a lab, who never had the wild streak attributed to my grandmother is grinning and waving at me.

"Now you!" She gestures to the first rock. With a glance at Doser, knowing that he can't save me from this, I set my satchel down beside mother's. The robot will bring both across with him. Assuming, we make it.

Water has always meant cleanliness to me, pure streams pouring from faucets, my shower, the swimming pools. Water isn't meant to have twigs and clouds of suspended mud swirling around my feet. Isn't meant to carry nasty critters and germs and other gross shit.

I remove my footwear and slide my bare feet into the disgusting water.

I move slower than mother, letting my body grow accustomed to the relentless pressure of the water surging around me, first my feet, then my ankles, then my calves. It's like being in a ball, dancing one of the more complicated patterns, the menagerie, where the group moves as one, the dancers tossed from partner to partner to partner, a dozen dances, all at once, shoulders brushing shoulders, the lines of movement constrained by the wall the dancers make of themselves.

I reach the first rock and though I want to climb it, rest, even live out my life on it, I do as mother has done, circling it and proceeding to the second.

I slip.

Drowning is such a subtle event; I'm barely aware of it. My knees, facing downriver, are buckled by the surging water, as if kicked from behind. This sends me falling forward, my head slipping under the churning waters.

Water rushes down my throat. Water pounds my shoulders, keeping my head under. Water grabs my feet, tugging me towards the falls.

Mother seizes me by my hair, tugging so hard that my scream would've been heard for kilometers if I were not underwater. As I rise to the surface, I'm connected to the rock she's using for support via her arm. She reels me in.

As I rise from the water I kick with my legs, and find purchase on the river's bottom. Mother's painful hold on my scalp loosens as I support my own weight, as I clamber to the rock and crawl onto it.

She vacates the rock as I scramble onto it and does not even ask me if I am okay. Just tells me to keep my knees pointed upriver.

"Upriver, got it," I say, spitting out another mouthful of water. I'm drenched, my hair so heavy it is almost painful. I roll into a ball on the rock and watch mother move from our rock towards the third, which is almost halfway across the river. Only a slight hump of rock rises from the water. Mother reaches for it, her hands curling over an outcropping that juts off the side of it.

I do not hear the rock crack and crumble but mother's cry of shock is piercing as she's swept away. For the briefest of moments my eyes meet hers and I won't ever forget what I see. Mother is not frightened, not in the least.

She's surprised.

CHAPTER 11

Carry Me To Ruin

Mother is surprised. Surprised because she's never considered herself fallible. She believes in her own myth, in the legend of the women of Terrasta. That we are indestructible.

I leap after her, without a thought. Maybe I do not have time for fear, maybe it's because of what I did (or didn't do) to help Adira. I just act.

The water is no warmer than before but I barely notice the temperature, it carries me swiftly and there's no fighting it; the flow foils my attempts to rescue mother as she's just rescued me. She's a dark blur against the light green waters, ahead. And the distance between us is increasing. Big Sister is dead. Little Sister might still draw breath but whatever of her life remains is hardly worth the living. And now mother will drown.

Doser saves me this time, his claw tangling in my hair and yanking hard enough to prod me towards the shore until I scramble onto the wet rock. I don't rest, I start off, chasing after mother, bare feet and all, but if she was a smudge before, she's a speck now.

The roar of the waterfall grows ever louder; I've rushed far enough downstream that I cannot see our packs anymore. I'm crying and flailing my arms, my chest heaving with the effort of the sustained run. Certainly not a glamorous, heroic moment, especially not with my occasional yelp when my heel is sliced from the jagged outcroppings of crumbling rock.

Basically, I'm a shambling, bleeding mess by the time the gorge twists away from me, my path ending; mother plummeting over the falls. I drop to my knees. She's dead.

Doser whirls to a stop above me.

"Well, that was unexpected." I glare at the uncaring lump of wood and steel. He doesn't have the programming to make him care.

I'm all alone now. There's nobody here to save me.

I'm weeping, really weeping, arms over knees, crying as I wait for Doser to fly upriver and retrieve our gear. Then he treats my bleeding feet best he can and urges me to pull my socks, then my boots, on. I do that, staring at the two satchels I have, at the extra pair of boots I have, when Doser asks me the question, the *important question*.

"Where to, now?"

Whatever sun was here earlier is hidden behind clouds, as if swept away with mother, but I'm oblivious to the light rain, to my discomforts. I'm stuck somewhere in my tangled thoughts. A few minutes or hours later he tries again.

"We need to cross."

Reluctantly, I nod. I know. But there'll be no more swimming for me. We have to continue north.

I walk past where mother started her ill fated swim. Mother has never listened to me, not ever. Nothing I've ever uttered mattered to her. And now there's no chance that I might rectify that. The dead cannot change, not even in our memories.

Except for my few minutes hiding inside the bushes, watching the attack on Kal, I've never been inside a forest, a real one that wasn't planned and choreographed by a professional. How to describe the way those trees loom over us? How their limbs claw at the sky, as if willing (and able!) to shred those clouds and reveal the obscured sun. Or if not able, at least desperate to try. And if their claws might not find their sun, will they turn upon us, the hapless fools who have stepped into their forest unbidden?

My grandmother and my mother, are dead. All I have left of them is grandmother's ashes in my satchel, alongside mother's tablet. For food and drink there's two food bars and a half full bottle of water. On the forest's fringe, before the trees become *really* thick and frightening, I drink most of the water and eat a bar. Then we hug the right side of the forest and try to keep the river in sight. I stumble along, mostly lost in my thoughts, my unspent grief.

Around midday I emerge from my funk long enough to ask Doser what he and mother had been talking about, earlier. "You wanted to go to Landing and mother wouldn't let you. Why?"

He pauses, and I stop as he regards me a full two seconds. "I suppose there's no harm in your knowing now. Your mother was worried for my safety."

"Worried? About you? Why?"

"Landing might not be secure."

Again I think of the men I saw below, right before the crash. The other clan? "She thinks our enemy has taken it?"

Only after I say the words do I realize I'm speaking of her in the present tense, as if she is alive. I'm not sure how many years it is going to take to rectify that mistake. How can a goddess die? How is that possible? But is… was… she right? I saw *somebody* on the island. Have savages crossed the bay and overcome Landing's crew? Stolen their weapons and turned the seeders against us?

It seems impossible. And why would they bother? The savages have nothing to complain about: food is plentiful and they suffer no illnesses.

Yet if mother believed it possible….

"Smoke," Doser says. I glance where he points, to the west. A thick dirty-black column rises and merges with the sky, as if it is an inferno, and not mother's machines, that creates Terrasta's clouds.

"We should backtrack, to the river," Doser says.

I bite my lip. If Landing has been compromised I'll be no safer there, than here. I stare at the smoke. Easier if mother were here to make this decision for me.

"Kal said his clan might be near." I'm whispering to myself but Doser has ears like God.

"You cannot be serious."

"What other option do we have? *If* the fire belongs to Kal's people, I might find protection among them, a way even, to rescue Adira. We cannot do that on our own." I make the point as if it was not already obvious to the robot.

"It might be the same clan that took her."

"Or Kal's! Or another! We don't know, Doser. We don't know!" I wipe at the soreness in my eyes, but I think I'm too exhausted to even cry. I just want things back to normal. That's all I want. I must do *something*: it's not like my situation could get any worse, right?

"Better if we remain on our own, Miranda. This planet is not safe."

"Not safe? No shit. But I'm tired. I'm cold." And I'm frightened. "I don't want to be on my own."

"We cannot risk this."

While I weigh the choices the wind picks up and tosses pellets of chill water against me. There's smoke and the possibility of a warm fire to the west. And I'm a human and Doser's only a robot. He has to listen to me.

Our walk is interrupted only by periodic breaks, but I stop bothering with even those once I exhaust my supply of food. By day's end it is only a monotonous trek towards the smoke. There's rain again, big *fatass* raindrops like you wouldn't believe. I'm wet and grouchy but I allow myself the faintest hint of a smile when I see mother's berries.

I drop to my knees before them, spilling rain water from the leaves as I tear fruit from the bush. These are beefier than mother's and maybe not quite as blue but I pop them into my mouth.

(Really, I have no choice, I'm but a slave to my stomach.)

"Yuck!" I cry, my voice echoing back at me from the surrounding trees as I spit magenta fluid and skin out. My mouth freezes, my tongue growing numb, like during a dental appointment.

"Some berries are poisonous," Doser says. My tongue won't move and I'm unable to say something nasty to Mr. Obvious. Instead, I'm forced to hurl the remainder of the offensive berries at him. They splatter and spoil his pristine appearance and now he looks like me:

124

shabby and miserable.

He shifts, midair, as if trying to shake himself free of the berry guts. It doesn't work and I take some delight in that, though I'm more concerned as a half hour of walking passes and my tongue still isn't working properly. It's not until the sun is low on the horizon that I'm able (after a fair bit of exertion) to speak.

"Gettin' close."

"You think?"

I kinda wish I had me more of those berries, I think, but he's right. The smoke is a thick column now and we are standing on a slight ridge, just to the north of it. When I catch my first glimpse of our destination though I hesitate, Doser doing the same, though I doubt he's as awestruck as I am.

I release a long, low gasp as I stare through the gaps in the trees at the clearing they hide, below us. The trees arc overhead, their great limbs touching, rising like the ceiling of Saint Parsons back home. This is a natural, rustic, cathedral; if filled with sunshine it might have been beautiful, even glorious, but in the soggy gloom it is anything but. Gray covers everything, as if a melancholy god painted the scene.

All that grayness only makes the rising mound of white moonrock in the center more vivid. This is a piece of the dead moon that must have flown wide of the rest and landed here, instead of in the bay. It stands twice as high as a man and at least five or six times wider. Its top is tapered, almost to a point; it resembles a teardrop.

There's more strangeness too. Tightly woven strands of fiber are tied between the trees, looping and crossing the clearing a dozen different ways. Below that web work the undergrowth is covered with the crushed remnants of skulls and leg bones and other, unidentifiable pieces.

This clearing is an important place, to somebody. And it is not unoccupied. Not only is there the smoke but I also hear voices. Still I can't see anybody, or the fire fueling the smoke.

"They must be around the other side of that rock," I whisper. The outcropping is large enough to hide a small group. I don't want to walk down and announce myself without knowing who they are so I crawl along the perimeter.

You'd think that the ground here might be more or less clear of gross critters, right? Wrong. There's crawling things everywhere and of all sorts, some have eight legs and others only six and yet others with so many tiny feet tucked up under their candy colored shells I can't count them. Worst of all are those without legs at all, the slithering things. Inadvertently, I slide my hands over them, recoiling when I touch their squishy, wet, squirming, bodies.

(I'd give anything, you know, for a concrete sidewalk.)

Every movement creates more noise than it

should, every branch I pass, snaps back into position with loud whistling and each time I cringe and pause. Doser remains silent above me, the robot knowing as well as I that we must make no sound unless we betray our presence.

The voices are louder as I pass the great flank of the white stone, but I still cannot make out words. The speakers are men, I know that much, and there's more than one of them. Their deep, rumbling voices remind me of Kal.

Something thick and coiled falls from the tree beside me.

I glance down at it, staring in shock as green and black muscle coils around my wrist, tightening. Two tiny eyes stare at me from a wedge shaped head. The dry, scaled body, makes two, then three, loops around my arm.

Do not scream, do not scream.

I smack it across the face.

The tiny mouth opens and I think it is going to bite me and no matter how hard I try not to, I know I'll scream if it does. But then Doser's there. He grasps the creature's head in his pincher as I backpedal and crawl away like a crab.

Do not scream.

I have to think this over and over, until Doser is able to unravel the snake. Then my robot spins several fast and concentrated circles until he has accelerated enough to toss the *snake* far away.

A snake. I don't think they even exist on Earth anymore, outside of the Bible. And thank,

God, really.

We resume moving and soon the voices are loud enough I recognize them. They do sound like Kal. They are his killers.

At the moment of my discovery I've angled far enough past the edge of rock that I see that the facing of the rock (previously hidden to me) curves inward, forming a nose to toes depression, wide enough for a couple men to fit in. Except there are no savages standing inside it. Nuzzled into that hollow part is a bed of burning bones.

The savages are standing in a line, their backs to me, staring at the pyre.

How anything can burn in this wet forest I don't know but the wood is piled high beneath the corpse. Smokey, pungent smelling flames rise, but I'm not looking at them, I'm focusing on the men, instead. Specifically the man from the beach, with his cruel eyes; the Savage. Their faces would have been invisible in the almost-darkness of twilight but illuminated by the firelight's flickering flames their features are harsh and jagged and monstrous.

Kal's head sits on a rock behind them, along with all their piled gear but there's no sign of Adira. I hope they have tied her somewhere close by. I might still rescue her; they won't hear me moving through the bush, not with the roar of the fire and their own muttering.

The Savage does most of the talking, though at times he hesitates, glancing at the older man, who then offers a word or gesture, which the younger mimics. Definitely a ceremony.

"Is that Kal's—"

I shush the robot, whispering to him, explaining what I'm seeing, who these men are.

"We must leave." The robot flies low enough that even though I'm crouched, he is still at eye level with me. I'm nodding at that when there's a boom of thunder and a half second later such a flash of light that it appears day has returned early.

The clearing becomes bright enough to see open sores on the oldest man's face. Now the man resembles a monster from the horror vids my brother used to make me watch. I don't remember him looking sickly before but I hadn't really paid much attention either. But I don't have time to figure that out now because I finally realize what burns on the pyre.

Adira.

They've sacrificed my little sister.

In that split second of light from the heavens, my body trembles and I fight to stop a scream from rising, from erupting. It doesn't matter, I realize, as the light starts dimming. I've done more than see. I've been seen. The Savage stops his speaking, his hard, animal eyes on me.

Then it's dark again.

I rush past the bushes, running blindly, not caring that I'm making noise. Noise doesn't matter now. They know I'm here. *He* knows I'm here. The rain slashes at me, as violent as the branches I barrel past. Between the forest and the downpour I'm cut and wet, a pale pink line of blood above my right eye, slowing me 'cause I have to wipe at it to see.

Damn this planet. It doesn't even have a proper moon, with proper light. And with my heart beating and the trampling I'm doing to the undergrowth I'm not hearing much either.

There's several more flashes of lightning, a series of them as if God is choreographing the chase, as if my terror is of amusement to Him. The thunder pounds the world, thick and deep bass like a commoner's souped up truck stereo and I shriek, it is so sudden and heavy, the sound like a thick blanket being thrown over my head.

Through it all I never stop running, not even when an arrow thuds into the thick trunk of a tree ahead of me and I have to skitter sideways. I risk a glance but see nobody. A wild shot, that is all. But a wild shot will kill as surely as any other.

Somebody is trying to kill me.

That just doesn't happen on Earth.

At least the rain is washing away the tears, letting me pretend that I'm not bawling my head off in terror and grief and utter exhaustion. Letting me pretend I'm braver than I am. Letting me pretend my legs are not near the point of collapsing.

I'm trying to run towards the river, more than willing to hurl myself into it. Better that then letting the savages take me. But when the river does not materialize after a few minutes of running I start to look instead for a place to hide. I'm too exhausted to run further.

The suffocating canopy of entwined limbs and leafy branches, has to be good for something, I think. I need a nook or cranny where I might tuck myself up, be as snug as a bug. The men might not search long for me, not if they are sick. I might hide, a day, a night, till they tire of the search.

I never should have followed the smoke; I should have risked it all instead on Landing. That's what mother would have done. I suppose that is what mother *had* done.

There. A cluster of five, maybe six, trees have fallen together, victims of some past lightning strike. I dive towards them but before I'm able to pull my head under it I stop because I hear *them*.

Not my pursuers. The bugs. I stare at my would-be hiding place and watch the bugs move. They are a mass of shadow only marginally darker than the darkness of everything else, as if shadow itself hides under logs at night.

There's clacking and crinkling and it is horrible, but I pull myself under, over top the mass of writhing insects. I'll be safe here until tomorrow and no matter how disgusting this all is, the bugs falling free or scuttling into my hair and down my face, I keep on crawling, crawling, crawling. I'm a tiny bug myself, burrowing to safety.

It is not to be.

Before I'm completely under I hear the Savage's voice again and then a strong hand grasps my ankle.

With a savage jerk, I'm pulled out.

CHAPTER 12

Grandmother's Ghost

Hi there, Mr. Durand! I'm fine, how are you? I trust that you'll pass my hellos onto Junira and Marcus. Thank you. I have no messages from Viv or Adira or mother. They are… indisposed.

Please accept my apologies for the poor quality of this video message. You are probably wondering why the image is dark and you can't see me. I'm sitting far from the camera, Mr. Durand, and there's not much in the way of light in this place.

Do not be alarmed. Just part of my mysterious, allure.

No lights, I imagine you are saying to yourself. Where in the universe might Miranda Terrasta find herself that she has no freakin' lights? Well there's the irony, I suppose, Mr. Durand, my love, and the only true light I need in this life. See, I'm marooned with your pets.

Have you ever seen them? They have names, of course, but I enjoy fabricating my own. There's Stumpy and Hangtooth and One Eye, and... and... well, there's others too. But why waste our time talking about them? No point to that. They're just savages; not real people. What they do, it doesn't matter. Not really.

Tonight I'm feeling like a damsel and you, as always, are a prince. I hope it doesn't alarm you, my thinking of you in this way. Though I suppose if you are a prince, maybe I'm a damsel in need—

Silly me, rattling on. None of this is coming out right. Please, Mr. Durand, do not worry. I've never been as wise or resourceful as mother wanted but be assured that I'm not stupid either. I'm watching. I'm learning. I'll choose my allies well. I'll survive.

Mother said we'd have an adventure and she never told a lie in all her life.

Oh, look, at me, I'm still blabbering on, am I not? Good thing this robot that's recording all this doesn't have opinions, because I'd fear what he'd think of me, though not nearly as much as I fear what you might think. No, I haven't gone mad, though I suppose if I had, I wouldn't know, would I?

(No, Doser, shut it. I'm talking now. And yes, it's important.)

Anyways, Mr. Durand, since I'm rattling on anyways, I wonder if you remember a girl named Juli? See, I told you about her, last fall.

Juli drifted, you know, always on the meds and when she wasn't, she should have been. I don't know what happened to her after she was dismissed from school but

I'm wondering now if I was missing out. Not that I was all proper and behaved, but I always steered clear of the wrong drugs, more or less. Now I'm really regretting that. From what I heard, Juli never had to remember anything. She lived day to day, without her past. I'm liking the idea of that.

Except then I'd forget about you and that'd be wrong. But everything else; I could do with not remembering that.

Whatever, right? I'm being silly. I just really miss you, Mr. Durand, and I wish I might hear your voice. I don't even have videos of you anymore, lost them.

Well, that's that. Hope life is treating you well.

All my love, my prince,

Miranda.

The bruises are mostly gone now but I don't want Salva to see what remains of them, don't want him to worry about me. I don't know if anybody from civilization will ever find me again, if Salva will ever find the messages, but just in case, you know.

Doser and I don't meet often, he's hiding out in the Fens, where the women dump the pisspots each morning, but when we do meet, this is what I do: talk to my past. Vid recording is about the only thing Doser is good for now that he's depleted his drug supply. Oh sure, he's tried talking me into fleeing, but what would be the point of that? The Savage and his clan have taken everything that ever mattered to me. Even grandmother's ashes.

This is my life now.

If One Eye notices I've slipped out of his bed of hides for an hour, he doesn't say anything when I slide back in, with him. I run my hand through my hair, hair that barely flows past my neck now. Some mornings I regret cutting it, but after... after everything that happened, I really didn't need it burdening me anymore. Cutting it, that was like making a clear break between the Miranda-I-Was and the Miranda-I-Must-Be.

I wince, I have another headache. Withdrawal from Doser's drugs is a bitch.

I avoid touching One Eye, but there's not much room under the hides. After my initial *welcome* into the clan, I now rotate when the moon completes a cycle, moving from lodge to lodge. One Eye's cramped home is my second since my capture, though the initial weeks of my stay (assigned to the man I call Stumpy) were spent on the march to here, their village. We are west of where our shuttle crashed, where my sisters and my mother died.

Where I was captured.

I close my eyes even knowing I might fall into dreaming again. At least I never dream about the capture itself.

The village of the Clan of Three Rivers reeks of cedar. The buildings, if they deserve such a mention, are built from tree logs and each lodge is arranged around a raised clearing. Only the headman's lodge is larger; it overlooks the others from a hill set in the center of the village.

It is strange, the dreaming, because I am both Mirandas. The one I was then, still stunned and dazed by all that has happened, and the other Miranda, not more than a month older but years wiser.

The adults pay no attention, most of the women staying inside their lodges, peeking out from the hides that serve as doors. If my step is too slow Stumpy prods me with his spear; I don't give him many opportunities.

It is only the children who watch, who study my face, and make eye contact. I'm not sure what they search for. I don't smile for them; I have no reason to bring joy to any savage. They are their parent's children after all and if my unusual appearance frightens them that's better for me.

I march through their ranks, keeping my eyes on the ground, watching my feet, not knowing where I'll be led. Then I hear the laughter.

I'd have expected it of savage men but when I glance I catch sight of three young women, on the cusp of adulthood. Their hands are over their mouths as if that token nod to propriety hides the sheer inappropriateness of their mirth.

They know what I have suffered and what I continue to suffer and it amuses the cruel girls.

Morning always comes too early, with One Eye demanding food and me scrambling awake to oblige him. As I stir the coals in the hearth, and fumble for the salty meat, left over from the night before, and heat it for him, I wonder if that cruel laughter was more relief than true mirth. The girls were not delighting in my degradation; they were grateful my fate was not theirs. With me here they are outside the attention of the men of the clan for a while.

The village is quiet and I do not think this has anything to do with my arrival. The hunters have brought more than me with them; plague has struck. An impossible plague. Salva had always insisted that the savages suffered from no illnesses. They should not be so sick but yet they are.

Nobody has died yet and two have recovered. But the headman, the Savage's father, is still ill. His son has been performing the old man's duties. *If* the man dies I tremble to think what will happen. His son will become headman and if my living hell could possibly become any worse, it will.

The Savage, he hates me.

Not just him. Many blame me for the sickness. Blame me because I'm not covered with the pustules, those sticky red wounds that mar the face and the body and if the moans of the afflicted are any indication, they hurt as much as they itch. The sick scratch themselves until their skin bleeds. So far only the older men and women are afflicted.

Even now as I mix the gruel to supplement the meager breakfast, I see, through the open flap of my hide doorway, a middle aged woman across the commons, whose name I do not know. She glares at me as she performs the same duties as I and I know it is because her mother is sick.

Two children rush out from behind her to join a handful of other children; all that the clan has. No child I've seen is younger than five or six. Several young couples have no children at all.

One Eye's shadow falls over me. For a moment it is as if he regards me with the puckered flap of flesh sewn over his right eye but then he turns his head, his gray-blue orb fixing on me as he sweeps his dull blond hair over his shoulders.

"Last meal." He reaches past and grabs the meat from the fire, not flinching, as if the heat means nothing.

I stare at him. "Already?"

"Eyes down," he growls and I obey, not wanting another beating. I want to ask him where I'm going but I know the other man will come for me when it is time. I ladle the gruel with a wooden spoon into a bowl carved from a section of tree. I've watched women working these bowls, scraping them with stone until they are polished as smooth as any ceramic bowl I've eaten from.

After he carries his meal outside to eat it with the other men, I pack, rolling the clothing they've given me inside a section of hide (my own satchel was taken with the ashes). The clothing mother made me wear… it is gone, and I haven't seen it since. During the entire march to this village I wore only the sheet of hide I now use to wrap the clothing they've given me into. My feet have long stopped bleeding, calluses growing over my much abused flesh. I suppose in time I'll be callused, mind and body.

Who will they send me to?

I have not lived in the Savage's lodge yet and though he already has two wives, I know I'll have to serve him, eventually. It is their custom; I'm their slave, their plaything.

"Please, not yet," I murmur. I need to be stronger before that happens, else I'll break, I know it. I'll make a mistake and he'll drag me out and kill me.

And would that be so bad?

"Maybe not," I whisper, replying to the voice in my head. Better if I had drugs, like that girl Juli from the world I never should have left. Drugged, I might slip away and become a zombie. Zombies don't *feel*. Don't wake in the morning after a sleepless night of terrifying nightmares. Don't worry that a single wrong gesture or word earns a bloody nose or a kick to the ass.

Zombies don't worry about whose bedskins they'll have to warm.

The Savage approaches One Eye and I watch them talk in low voices. I shudder. He shall be my next keeper, I just know it, I just dread it.

"Protect me, grandmother," I whisper across the commons, my voice following One Eye, but snaking past him, into the Savage's lodge. *That night* he took her ashes from me. She's inside there, already, with him. Waiting for me.

But maybe, just maybe, my upcoming

torments will offer some reward. Unlike One Eye, the Savage has wives. Surely they will tell me what happened to my poor sister, Adira. This has gnawed at me since I was taken. Why do I live and she does not? And so I wait, tidying One Eye's house so I won't be accused of laziness.

Not knowing my fate, it is the worst.

CHAPTER 13

How a Gal Copes

Before I am consumed by worry, a woman who is not a wife of the Savage, emerges from a lodge near the village's edge. She's wearing a long dress like mine, made of softened deer hide, though where my dress is plain, hers has pretty beadwork along the cuffs and down the sides. Her hair is capped by a skin cap, though I do not think this is so much due to custom as to the almost persistent drizzle.

She stops in front of One Eye's lodge.

"Come."

She's not staring at the ground as she might have if I were a man but she's not meeting my eyes either. I suppose accepting another woman into her home, her husband's bed, is awkward.

"I'm Miranda," I say as I follow her across the courtyard.

"Zamora." Physically she doesn't seem any

different: her skin is pale and the few strands of hair peeking from the cap are the color of straw. But though I have given my own names to the savages, I have paid attention to their true names and know that hers is unusual.

They've staked Kal's head not far from Zamora's lodge, right beside the trail leading to the Fen. Despite the rains the weather is warm enough to be unkind to the flesh remaining on his skull and insects cover it, walking in and out of the empty eye sockets with impunity.

Zamora pulls her hide door aside and I enter ahead of her. She follows and tugs her wet cap off, freeing a mass of blond hair. The woman is around my age, I realize.

Two candles sit on a crude table made from bark stripped logs and they are the only light; the hearth fire mere embers. Beside the candles are a wooden box, curious because care has been taken in its construction, the wood worked by a skilled carver.

"What's this?" I ask, as I stop beside the table.

"A marriage box," she says, running her fingers over the carved surface. "Given to me by my husband's mother, before her soulspirit was set free. It should have been my mother who did this but that was not possible."

"Why not?" I ask, though I am also busy examining what will be my home for the next month. This lodge is cleaner than One Eye's and there's even a few carpets, woven from reeds. The beams running overhead have hooks carved into them and blankets and bark pots and herbs hang from them. A woman's house is more of a home than a bachelor's. I suppose some things do not change, no matter how far away from Earth we might be.

"I wasn't born here."

"Where are you from?"

She gives me a look and I know she does not want to talk about this and I drop the subject. I'm feeling the first tug of, well, not quite happiness, but a respite, I suppose, the dreariness I've been suffering since captivity being nudged aside, for now. Zamora and I share common ground and I dream that might lead to friendship.

The day passes and though I learn on which mats I am to sleep and where the food is stored and how Zamora wants to divvy up the chores I do not learn who her husband is. She calls him Otu but the name means nothing to me.

I glance often at the marriage box. On Earth the customs in the west have remained unchanged for generations. I'd have been given an engagement ring by the man who asked for my hand (presumably Salva) and then later, at our marriage, we'd exchange marriage bands. Here it appears that a bride's mother packs a box full of clothing and mementos of her childhood and the bride carries that into her new home.

When I'm not tidying up or pacing I'm glancing outside. A streak of spring sunlight warms the common ground between the lodges and the savages take advantage of the warmth. Their lives are nothing like what I'm used to. There's more variety in their skin tones than back home where we've all been cut from the same genetic cookie cutter, though none are as dark skinned as I. Not all are blond either, there's also black and brown hair and even hints of red which hasn't been seen on Earth in four or five generations.

It is fascinating and horrifying, all these differences. I wonder that the people find anything at all to talk about. How can you help pick clothing for a person who does not look like you? How can you advise on the right shade of makeup or a blouse or a dress?

Not that it matters here. Not really. The woman are attractive enough but it's not as if they actually compete for the attention of the men. Marriages are business transactions, hardly matters of love.

Otu returns homes at dusk and when he steps into the lodge I recognize him. He's the man who spoke against the attack on Kal, on the beach. He grunts a greeting, then turns his back to me, to eat his evening meal beside Zamora.

Otu does not climb into my hides that first night, the next, or even the night after that. He seems content to be with Zamora, instead and it is as if I am invisible to him. Throughout the next week the man barely speaks a word to me.

Tonight there's another frenzied party outside. The savages enjoy their celebrations and they leap at any excuse to act as wild as many Earthlings imagine them to be. I part the hide door and glance outside, at the revelers. The party is in honor of a child's first laugh. The boy seems a tad old to have waited this long, but what do I know of savage ways? He sits at the place of honor, around the great bonfire in the commons and beside him is Otu, the man who made him laugh. It is Otu's responsibility to host the feast and Zamora and I spent the day preparing the meat and soups and breads the clan now enjoys.

I was not invited to the party.

Still I smile, at the sheer mirth the clan exhibits, as if the boy's first laugh somehow is contagious and all of them, even the dour Savage and the headman, who both sit to Otu's left, laugh with him.

Even these savages, I suppose, are human.

The headman leans toward Otu, as they watch the women, whom are dancing and singing on the far side of the fire. The men share another whispered conversation, just one of many I've seen tonight. Zamora talks often (and with pride) of the respect the headman has for her husband, and I see that she has not inflated her opinion of him.

If this is to be my life, until my rescue, I might bear it. Except that in another month I'll be thrown to another man. I doubt I'll find a reprieve such as Otu's again for respites are rare on Terrasta.

Even spring is not as pleasant as she should be. Most days are wet and overcast and today was the worst. The rains stopped a few hours ago, about the same time that the clan's magician arrived (she's a strange old lady who does not live in the village itself). The clan believes the song she used to start the feast also stopped the rains.

(They are all fools. The only woman on this planet who was capable of controlling the weather is dead.)

Thunder rumbles, in the distance, but I do not smile. I've been sitting here and trying to build up the courage to sneak out and meet with Doser, who I have not spoken to since moving to Otu's lodge (a drawback of having two women in a lodge is that I am never alone, when I walk to the Fen to dump the pisspot). A rainstorm would only send the clan scurrying back to their lodges.

The headman rises, Otu and the Savage helping him stand, and the dancing, the singing changes, slowing down. He stares back at them, a long moment, and then with the Savage's help, he is escorted to his lodge. Only when he disappears inside does the party resume.

What drones: they lack individuality and rely too much on one another. The savages are stuck in time. They will never break through their chains of conformity, never advance beyond the primitive.

I watch the celebration a few moments more

but there is not going to be a better time than this, to slip away, for an hour or two and so, resolved, I slide on the leather slippers Zamora has given me and throw a leather wrap over my shoulders.

I step away from the warmth of the hearthfire and enter the darkness. The night is chill but my clothing keeps me comfortable. Back on Earth I'd never consider myself capable of wearing the skin of a dead animal but I find that such convictions have no weight in the reality I am faced with.

I lift the pisspot (needing an excuse to walk to the Fen) but my brave walk almost ends before it begins because I stumble into Zamora. She's standing not far from our lodge in front of the stake holding Kal's head.

For the celebration, several torches have been erected on the ends of long shafts of wood hammered into the ground and though everything is in shadow, none of us are invisible. She does not notice me immediately. Sweat, from her exertions, dancing with the other women, still trickles down her forehead but she's not thinking about music or rhythm right now. She's whispering as she stares at Kal's head; I do not hear her words.

"Zamora," I say, intruding on whatever she is doing here, but not wanting to startle her as I walk past — and walk past I must, for the path to the Fen curves around her. She glances at the pisspot and gives me a strange sort of shrug before hurrying back to rejoin the dancers. I want to know what she was doing here but calling after her will only give her reason to ask why I'm heading to the Fen with an empty pisspot.

I had hoped we might have grown closer but she's as aloof as Otu and barely speaks with me.

Thunder barks, still far enough away but not so far that I don't think back to the night the savages captured me. It is as if I associate the storm itself with what happened after the capture and it almost makes me turn back.

The Fen sits to the southeast of the camp, just off the crossroads. If I were to march straight ahead I might take the trail away from this valley itself but instead I turn right, into the sprawl of stunted trees that ring the marshy Fen. I stop after a few steps because I hear voices ahead, and see a ball of light, through the branches. It is a torch. There is somebody here.

I glance at the pisspot. I *must* speak with Doser. Eventually the beaten down grass of the trail transitions into rock. Stones have been placed over the damp marsh, generation after generation, until a proper raised trail leads into a clearing. To either side of me is the Fen, with its wet, slithering things, and around the final curve of the trail, on a slight hill at the far end of the clearing, is a small lodge. This place, that reeks of the shit and urine dumped into the Fen, is where the women are exiled during their menses. I have yet to notice any woman use it, since I've come here, but it would not surprise me that the torchlight I saw earlier belongs to a woman inside the dwelling.

I am wrong.

There are three women standing about halfway between where I am and where the lodge is. None carry pisspots, but one has a torch. The women are joking and laughing and I see that two carry clay drinking vessels.

I relax somewhat; they've only come here for a break from the constant harassment of the males and the demands of their children. I'd never have thought of a bathroom as a sanctuary and it is yet another way in which Terrasta is alien. I steer as wide as possible away from the women.

But I am noticed and the conversation ends.

"Look at this. The dogwhore has slipped free of her kennel," The torchbearer says and I recognize her long face. She is the Savage's second wife. The three laugh, far too loudly than they should. Really, it isn't that amusing.

"Why are you here?" The Savage's first wife, asks. She's a year or two younger than me but the privilege of being the wife of the son of the headman has given her confidence. I lift the pisspot, but say nothing, as I stare at the ground. My heart beats wildly and I pray they accept the lie.

The other women start to taunt me but the first wife waves them away and steps toward me. I flinch when she raises her hand but all she does is touch my hair, strokes it.

"What life do you have left for you?" she whispers and I glance up. Her words are gently

150

spoken but there's insufficient light for me to judge whether she's sincere or teasing.

"What do you mean?"

"You, dogwhore, shall never have hearth or family. Better if you flee. Now. Tonight."

My eyes widen.

"I must not." I think of all the excuses I have given Doser previously. Where would I go? How would I survive? And worse: what would happen to me, if I am caught again. I could not survive it, I just couldn't.

Not that this woman cares. She laughs, her grip tightens on my hair, and I squeal as she rams my forehead against hers. "Kono does nothing but talk about you! He says he hates you, that you disgust him, but I would rather that *my man* not speak of you at all. Flee into the hills. Climb far and if they might catch you, then better death, than capture. Throw yourself from the cliffs. But do not come back to my village."

She releases me and I stagger back, blinking tears from my eyes. She wants me to flee, wants me to kill myself. Her motivations are selfish but maybe, she's not wrong. The trio walk away and take their light with them.

Before I have recovered, Doser floats out from the Fen, his lights dim so that he is almost invisible. I'm still too shocked by my confrontation with Kono's wife to startle.

"The bitch is right. Tonight, you must escape. I've found the way."

CHAPTER 14

Escape Plans

I know some of my friends think that rain is romantic but sitting on a damp log in a clearing smelling of excrement and talking to a robot? No rain is capable of rendering this scene the least bit romantic. Here, in this marsh, the rot that is taking hold of the trees is hard to ignore, splotches of white and yellow fungi covers their bark. Mother's plants and trees are dying but it is a slow death.

"I'll kill the watchers," Doser says with the same tone he might have used to tell me the temperature.

"What?"

"You may have been preoccupied, Miranda, but the trail we took to the village, it is the only way in, to this valley. Men guard the pass."

I nod, remembering. The scouts are unmarried men, and spend a week or two at a time, rotating shifts. Whenever a shift ends and a man returns is cause for a small festival. (I did say the savages like to party, right?)

"And... and you want to kill them?"

"Send them over the cliff and then you are free, Miranda."

I'll fly home, back to a world where the mere crack of thunder won't make me piss myself. "I don't want anybody to die."

"Then you don't want to escape."

I glare at him.

"I'm desperate to return home, Doser. I don't want to be here." There's more to life than wormy meat and stale grains and eternal blandness. I am not born for a life of drudgery, I am incapable of surviving it. I know this about myself.

But right now, with Otu, I'm not being mistreated. I'm being fed and clothed. I'm surviving. In the woods, with Gehum's monsters, there are no guarantees. And if I have to kill....

I try to explain this all to Doser but in the end he's only a robot and doesn't understand.

"In a few weeks you move to another man's lodge. And then another. And then another. You are Miranda Terrasta. This life is beneath you."

I nod but I'm near crying too. Here, am I really Miranda Terrasta anymore? I never should have survived all that has already happened.

"It is your decision."

Is it really a decision though? If I'm already starting to forget what being a Terrasta gal means, what will happen in another month, in a year?

"What other choice is there."

He answers me, as if I had actually asked a question. "I might proceed to Landing myself. *If* all is well there, I'll send a rescue party for you."

"No way." That was not an option for mother and it's less of one for me. How can I exist here without Doser? Without a reminder that there's a better world out there? It has to be this way, before I lose my nerve. "You are right. We must go. Now."

"Wait a moment. You will need supplies."

Shit. "I didn't think—"

"You must start thinking," Doser says and I almost imagine it is Viv or mother chiding me, as if a remnant of them exist inside the robot's shell.

I nod. "If the weather holds, the celebration will continue. I have time to sneak back and gather what I need. I'll meet you here, in an hour."

Doser considers all this in that silent way that is unique to robots and finally chirps in agreement. "And find the weapons they used against the shuttle."

I blink, not having thought about that at all. "If they are here... they'd be in Kono's hut."

"Kono?"

I blink, realizing I've used Kono's name for the first time with the robot and not the title of

154

Savage.

"He's the headman's son."

"Best to leave them there, then," Doser says but I know what he's thinking. Spears and arrows can't do much against Doser's armor but proper weapons might undo any chance of escape.

And don't forget my ashes. Grandmother's voice intrudes, as if she's standing there beside the robot.

"I won't forget," I whisper.

"What's that?"

I blink again. "Nothing." I don't tell him but I'll try to find the weapons (and the ashes). The more we stack the odds in our favor, the better my chances. If I'm going to escape, I'll do it properly. "The sooner we reach Landing… the Tower, the better."

I had asked Zamora about the place, the day after moving into her lodge. Now I try to explain to Doser what it means to them. That it is a holy place. That it frightens them and that I'm sure it is the key to all this. Once I reach it, this life ends, and my old life resumes. I'll forget this nightmare has ever happened and if I forget, then Salva, will never know.

On the walk back, alone, that part of myself that never existed back on Earth, reminds me that Landing, the Tower, might be no safer than remaining here. I tell her to shut up. I need some flicker of hope and the Tower must be it.

I say this over and over, muttering to myself.

By the time I reach the village, I am almost convinced.

The fire still roars, the flames still lick their logs. The tribe is calmer now, the music softer, a resonant song that seems to have lulled them all into a trance, even Kono, his massive frame at rest beside the fire. Otu is there still too and the women sway, before the flames, which whisper and hiss when the light rain touches them.

I decide to search the headman's home first but when I reach the threshold I pause. I've listened to the lectures the women give their children, and I know that stealing and hording are the worst of all sins for the clan, as is intrusion into their homes without permission.

I'm torn, standing here, part of me, the wiser part wanting to flee back to Otu's and accept my fate because *acting*, because making that choice to follow the pyre's smoke led me to capture. If I had headed towards the Tower instead, I might have been rescued. On the other hand, not acting, to save Adira, had caused her death.

I'm frozen between two choices, between doing nothing and suffering and doing something and suffering worse. If I am caught—

"I will not be," I whisper and then step into a room darker than the night behind me. I'm halfway across the floorboards, heading towards the far wall where there's a stack of woven baskets and woolen sacks, when thunder shakes the building. For the briefest of eternities I'm on my back and staring up at the looming faces. Stumpy. One Eye. Kono—

"Silly, Merry," I whisper. It is just a storm. If I do this, if I free myself from them, I'll never have to think about *it* again.

It only takes seconds for me to realize there are no rifles or rockets hidden here beside the baskets and sacks. They must be stashed elsewhere. But grandmother's ashes *are* sitting atop the mound of grain sacks.

I lift the urn, not needing to check to realize it has not been opened, for only I know the code. There is a long scratch down the side but the savage's tools are incapable of rending our metals. I press the urn against my chest, as if somehow, through this contact, I might be connected with that proud and feisty woman. Had she been in my situation, she would have turned the tables on these savages already.

"I'm sorry," I whisper. Then my gaze falls onto the sacks themselves. The lighting is dim but sufficient for me to see lettering. This alone should be enough to shock me, but it is the words themselves that set me to trembling.

Each box has a Terrastan seal and, in Courier (the official font of the universe) I read the date and time of packaging. But there is also other writing; this secondary text *appears* handwritten but is too uniform. A machine printed these.

Stay true to the Thunderbirds and our gifts continue;

dishonor us and you will be as the Birdeaters are. You will be carrion.

"Jesus Christ," I whisper. This can't be something mother's company has done. We don't even harvest grain here, just collect the seeds and sell them to large farming cooperatives on Earth. But who else? Gehum? Why would they feed the clans, why would they make their lives easier, when they claim that they are forcing them to survive on their own?

And why add such odd writing? I don't even know what a Birdeater is.

If the date of manufacture was from years ago, before Salva took the helm, I'd not have been surprised but this grain was packed well after he took control. I think back to our few discussions on religion, how he dismissed my family's belief in God, our sporadic attendance of Church (just the major holidays, thank you).

He called religious belief an abnormality, yet here his company is exploiting it, convincing savages that food comes from these Thunderbirds, whatever they are.

And who can read this? Not the savages, surely. There's another peal of thunder and no matter the importance of my discovery I must leave, now. Maybe Doser will make sense of this, later, but it is not my mystery to solve.

"Slave!"

I spin, urn still in hand, and see the old headman leaning against the centermost support pole. I'm a fool; I've forgotten he was brought here, earlier.

He coughs wetly. My mind churns, searching for a lie to extract me from the situation but I find none. He's an old, sick man, as frail as a scarecrow standing there. If I shove past him, I might still escape. Yet might I not do more? Behind him, in a basket, are the logs used to keep the hearthfire lit. They are no longer than my forearm but each is heavy. He smiles, seeing what I see. Can I do this? Can I strike an old man?

If not for the next round of thunder I might have tried but there's several blasts that shake the lodge and I'm back there, to the night of my capture with the men on me. I blink and I don't know how much time passes but then Kono's rushing across the lodge, lashing out, a punch that sends me to the floor.

"Kill her!" cries his wife.

CHAPTER 15

Unlikely Rescue

I'm a feather tossed by violent winds, thrown wall to wall, protecting my face more by instinct than any intent. The rain pounds the roof but I barely hear it above Kono's growls and my moans. Every time the thunder shakes the building I'm living through two nightmares.

"Dirty, thieving, dogwhore," Kono snarls. I'm prone with my arms and legs drawn around myself. I don't know what to say, and maybe, I can't say anything. Despite the shelter of the lodge this is too much like that other time; the storm is just as violent and unstoppable.

"Kono!"

The tall savage stops, staring behind, at where Otu and several other men have entered. I press myself against the sacks of food, dripping blood onto the wooden floor. The newcomers have carried torches into the lodge, and the room is all the brighter.

There's a silence and I have to turn my head to see why, to see that all the men are regarding me. I want to speak but I can't. The scent of so many men in so small a place is overwhelming.

I was not stealing, not really, but I'm still holding grandmother's ashes and there's no defense I can make.

"Stand up," Otu says and I obey, my back pressing against the stored goods, as if I might slip through the cracks between sacks and baskets and disappear. I'm trembling, the urn bouncing in my grip.

Otu strides across the room and strikes me with his broad hand. I'm back on my knees and he's grabbing me by the shoulder and dragging me towards the exit.

"Stop!" There's a different texture in Kono's voice; he's not raging anymore, whatever emotions are roiling underneath his skin are darker, subtler, crueler. "She must be punished."

"No," I whisper but there's a hesitation in Otu, and I know he's considering this. All the men are.

And then the birdwoman enters and if not for this I think my fate might have been the same as the night they captured me. The men scramble away from the entrance, like dancers parting for the main act. I'm shocked to see the men move like this for a mere woman.

She's tiny and wrinkled and ancient, her eyes buried in her folded flesh. In her youth she must have been a more robust woman and the

161

skin remembers. She's the clan's magician.

She's never spoken to me and I've never asked after her. To be honest I thought she was just some crazy old woman living on the camp's fringe, doing nothing more than feeding her birds. Even here, in the dead of night, there are several of the tiny creatures nesting on our shoulders. Her leather dress is a bright blue, the most colorful garment I've yet seen.

"Enough of this. This is a night of celebration," the birdwoman says, her gaze as stern as her voice. "It must not be marred."

"But she has stolen from my lodge, magician," Kono says, his tone almost deferential, like when he speaks to his father. She ignores him, gazing at the old man instead.

"And what did she steal?"

He's silent a long spell, though the weather outside prevents true silence. I'm still trying to shake the fuzziness from my head and I use my sleeves to mop blood from my face. This has not been covered in mother's speeches about Terrasta — none of us gals were taught to take a punch.

The old man points at grandmother's urn.

The birdwoman asks, "And this is yours?" He nods but before she turns her beady eyes to me, before she points a crooked finger my way, Otu speaks.

"We took that from her, when we captured her. It has significance, if she's risked this."

I flush. It *should* have had significance, if I were a better granddaughter. But his words are a lifeline, cast my way, and regardless of my guilt I know I have to hold onto it. With my eyes fixed to the floor, I tell the birdwoman what the urn holds.

"Ancestor ashes," she whispers but everybody hears her anyways, nobody else dares talk. A few back away.

Only Kono continues to glower. "Who cares—"

"We *must* care," the birdwoman says, stroking the head of a small black and blue bird, "else we dishonor our own soulspirits. This slave is merely taking back what is her responsibility."

"She should not have trespassed!" Kono's wife cries, as if she's worried that I'll yet live through this encounter.

"She must be punished," the other wife says.

"Has she not already been punished?" Otu asks and again I want to glance at him, to show my gratitude. I realize when he struck me earlier, it was his attempt to stop the situation from worsening.

Again there is silence, all eyes on the headman and I realize that despite her aura of authority even the birdwoman must still defer to his judgment. This is the culmination of all my fears, this is why I need to leave this wretched place. They have power over me and that is not right, not their right.

The storm has paralyzed me and now I am helpless. Like before. My fate, it seems, is to be helpless, here on Terrasta.

"I do not think she belongs here," the headman says, finally. "I do believe she'll cause troubles, that it would be best if she were—"

The birdwoman interrupts him. "The slave bleeds!"

Why that shocks the crowd, why that sends the men fleeing to the far side of the lodge, I don't know immediately. Of course I'm bleeding; I've been beaten. But then I glance down and realize what she is saying.

My body has contrived to save my life.

The sound of scurrying carries me from my troubled slumber and I wake, for the first time in ages, alone. I'm in the Fen, in the cramped lodge the women use during menses.

When I touch my face I wince and my world collapses again. I rise, body creaking, muscles stiff from abuse, and hobble to the hide doorway, parting the flap and cringing at the ripe odor of feces and urine. During the walk back last night, the birdwoman explained to me how the men feared our monthly blood flow.

"The godlings wage war inside women," she had said, "spilling our blood."

If I had not been groggy, from the beating, I might have questioned *why* the godlings would bother to battle inside a mere woman. Instead I nod, grateful to be free of Kono's influence, at least for a few days, and even more grateful that nobody had stopped me from hobbling out of Kono's lodge with grandmother's ashes.

I glance behind me, to ensure that the urn is still there beside the hide bedding that Zamora carried out for me. She didn't speak to me during the walk, insisting on staying several strides behind the birdwoman and then departing with only a nod.

I hear the scuffling again. I have no weapon (and if I did I wouldn't know what to do with it) so I keep within the threshold of the lodge and hold onto the doorway to lean around the side, surveying the land of my exile. I've slept late and it is almost noon, and the sun is almost bright.

"Good morning," the birdwoman says. I squeal in surprise and fall from the lodge, my bare feet landing in damp mud. She's sneaked up behind me. But as I stare, her eyes widen.

"Your face," she says.

I duck my head, embarrassed.

"No, no," she continues, the birds covering her, accenting her words with coos and hums. It is like a living carpet of winged things that crawls across her, pecking at her blue dress. "Not your injuries. Your face; it is not unfamiliar."

I blink at that, wondering if she might have seen my mother or grandmother, at some point in the past. Which is impossible. But she does not elaborate, instead pulling seed from her pouch and opening her hand so that several of the tiny creatures land on it and peck with a vigor I'm sure must hurt. But either the woman doesn't feel the pain or she doesn't care.

"Thank you, for last night." I am awkward, vulnerable, here on the edge of the doorway, mindful that at any moment other women of the clan might arrive.

The birdwoman shakes her head. "I did not help you. I did as the godlings commanded. You'd be best thanking them, instead." She lifts her finger, a beady-eyed black bird with an orange throat perched there. He's wears a lordly expression, as if her finger is his castle, and he is peering down upon all those under his dominion.

"The bird?"

She smiles, revealing a mouth devoid of tooth. "The godlings speak through the animals. He was compelled to find me, to tell me where you were. No woman of the clan has fought a blood war in years."

None of them are menstruating? I shudder as I realize the reason behind the lack of younger children.

"The godling told me a blood war was soon to begin, that you were entering the woman's time. *That* is why I came."

"That's not what you said, last night—"

"Because I alone hear the godlings's words, I am respected. But still, men seldom accept my words without proof. Without a sign."

"You were… stalling. But how could you have known I would…." I let the words trickle away and she knows she doesn't need to answer 'cause I've figured out what she'd say anyways. She'd tell me the godling told her.

She flicks the birds off and they scatter, landing on the lodge. She digs into her pack and retrieves strips of cured meat and a few carrots and we breakfast. I devour the meal, propriety taking a backseat to necessity.

"Where have you come from?" she finally asks. Nobody has expressed interest in this before though it must have been obvious to them that I'm not from a nearby clan. Not only is my skin darker, they've had to teach me things even children know. This old woman has a curiosity the others lack. Yet how can I explain rockets and longhaulers and jaunts to her?

"My clan is up there, past the Orphan," I say, using their word for moon.

Her hands covers her mouth. "That's not possible."

I think I've frightened her and we don't talk any more that morning until she reminds me that I am not to leave the area near the lodge. Then she trundles away.

So I'm alone.

And loving it.

"Ain't this the best, grandmother?" I pat the urn.

"Why do you keep birds?" I ask the birdwoman the next day.

She's sitting in the hut with me, sharing, like yesterday, a breakfast. The hide is open, letting in the warm sun and it's almost pleasant, though

I suspect the lack of men here has more to do with that than the weather.

The wind is blowing the stench of the Fen away from me this morning and bringing with it more pleasing odors; sun warmed pine and cedar. I flinch, remembering that the only reason I know the names of these trees is because of my dead mother's instruction.

"Keep them? I do not. They *come to me*, with their godling whispers." The old woman uses a gnarled knuckle to stroke the tiny head of the black and orange bird. The bird lolls its head back, trembling under her touch. "They are messengers and I'm obliged to care for them. No hunter may harm a winged thing, for if such harm is done, the godlings speak no more to the clan."

"That is why you don't eat birds." I've noticed the lack, even if back on Earth I'd hardly have paid attention.

I'm enjoying the conversation. Rest and isolation, I do not think these such bad things, though I initially ridiculed the idea of the women being isolated from the men. Now I understand why they have never protested this custom; it is a respite from the constant neediness of their menfolk.

"We respect our godlings. That's why the Birdeaters are worse than animals, are beneath us."

I listen while she tells me about this rival clan and I soon realize that she is talking about Kal's people. I burst out, "But they look like you!"

"They do not," she says, with a huff. "The differences are many. Did you know that their men can't grow proper beards? Or that they have difficultly mating?" She makes a crude gesture with her finger. I blush but also feel a heartpang for the gesture reminds me of the one Adira used, so long ago.

"It is because they eat the birds." I am, by this point, trying very hard not to laugh but her eyes are wide open with the same passion she demonstrates when speaking of godlings. The crazy old lady continues. "We used to live closer to them but they drove us off. Their cruel raiders stole our girls and boys; used them to sate their lusts." Her words bring true color to my cheeks. Does she not realize on how many levels what she says is hypocritical?

"As I was stolen?"

She shakes her head, wags a finger. "Our ways may seem harsh but they are fair. Zamora was taken, like you but now she is married. She has become a daughter of the clan."

My eyes widen and now I understand: Zamora stood beside Kal's head that night because she knew him. She was an outsider to this clan, too, but was eventually accepted into it. I understand what the birdwoman is trying to tell me but I do not accept it.

"We are not cruel like the Birdeaters. If you win a man's affections, you'll become his wife."

She's staring at me and I'm almost overcome by how birdlike her eyes are. They don't look old at all and I remember grandmother was like that, that when I stared into her eyes it was as if I saw the woman she had been. The woman of her youth, the woman I imagined she always dreamed herself back to.

The birdwoman has done me a kindness, offering me this. It is a kindness I don't know I want to accept. Tonight I intend to find Doser; I may lack supplies but after Kono's beating I can't stay here.

"Thank you," I say, looking away from her, at the floor.

"Is there a man who has caught your eye?"

I shake my head. "This is all too overwhelming."

"Yet you must accept it. And summer is shorter than you might imagine. The weather will turn soon."

"I don't... understand," I say, because clearly, I don't connect the weather with my situation at all.

"A woman alone will not survive. Find a husband and abandon further attempts to escape."

"I didn't—"

"The birds know," she says, holding out the black and orange one again. "Go on now, pet him."

I do as bid, because I don't know how I might refuse her and as I touch the feathers she says no more about my escape attempt. The bird is warmer than I anticipated. I stare at the old woman; she's cunning. Again, like grandmother.

The bird finally grows bored of my attentions, hop-walking up the woman's arm to nibble at a pouch of food around her neck. But as he abandons me I'm sure he glances my way and nods. I smile back.

"Otu is a capable man," the birdwoman says, as the visit draws to a close.

"He is," I say, for it is a truth. He is (almost) as good a man as a savage might be, though I'd have traded him in a heartbeat for Kal.

"Soon you'll move to another lodge." She does not need to say the rest. If I want Otu I have only a handful of days to convince him I'm a worthy bride. "And Kono will have you next."

CHAPTER 16

A Monster in the Swamp

The old woman has given me a lot to think about: settle for Otu (assuming he'd have me) or risk it all on escape? Her words churn through my mind and as night descends, I slip out of the lodge, in search of Doser.

I shiver, drawing the hide tight around my shoulders, the scraped leather rubbing against my neck. I don't want to stray far from the trail cutting through the Fen but I soon realize he is not hiding where he tends to and I worry about whispering his name, lest I am heard by a woman. Not that any should be here, this late, but one never knows what a savage will do, right?

Nobody must learn Doser exists for he is

my only true ally. The birdwoman, for all her sporadic kindnesses, is *one of them*. The leafs rustle and the branches quiver as I part them, peering into the darkness, on the verge of the Fen.

Where is he? Has he abandoned me? Has he fled to Landing?

I am stepping off the rock trail, my feet sinking into spongy, fetid, vegetation, when there's a splashing, not nearly far enough away. Then there's a snort followed by a second and I step back onto the trail. The trees in the distance waver, as if afraid, like me. After the third snort I flee back to the lodge, even thought the hide flap is not going to offer me much protection. (Why can't these savages build proper doors?)

I peek, as I did the other day with the birdwoman, my muscles straining to support me. Gradually the unusual noises dissipate and the horizon lights with the sun's rising. I venture out again. I would love to convince myself that what I heard had been my imagination but I soon discover thick clumps of fur covering several of the trees, just off the trail, as if a beast has rubbed against them.

Several of the clumps are out of my reach. I remember Doser saying how tall he thought the monster in the woods had been and I shudder. Surely such a creature has not entered Kono's valley?

There's a whoop-whooping and I pause, again. There is only one creature on all of

Terrasta capable of making such a noise and I know I've found my robot. It takes me almost a half hour but I follow his pathetic noises and finally find him, several meters inside the Fen proper, underneath a moss covered log. Mounds of green fronds and chunks of rotted wood have been dragged ashore as if some beast emerged from the Fen waters themselves.

"Doser?" I keep watch for whatever creature made last night's noises. I'm far enough into the Fen that I cannot see the lodge anymore and I shuffle forward, timid and nervous.

His eye lights when I'm within reach of him but I leap back as his claw slashes at me.

"Hey! It's me."

The claw thrashes the ground a couple more times but with some cajoling Doser emerges. I gasp. There's a gash through his mahogany shell, a full chunk of it torn free. The control board inside his skull is strobing through all the colors of the rainbow and really I shouldn't be seeing that at all.

"Sorry," he says. It take him some effort to float upwards, so that we are of the same height. The clanking of his machinery is loud enough that I reach and hold him in place so he doesn't have to fly.

His camera eye whirls as he studies my face. "I hope," says he, "that I don't look as bad as you."

"Kono did this," I explain, but he chirps as if Kono is insignificant.

"Well, a *monster* found me." Doser explains

that one of Gehum's genetic monstrosities did indeed attack him. He had been struck, damaging his repulsers and barely making it under the log. There he has hid, giving himself time to undo the worst of his injuries. Doser, like all robots, has the capacity to repair himself, but the damage done was significant.

"It will take some time and I won't ever be whole again."

(Gee, I know how that is!)

I tell him what happened to me, all the while scanning for signs of the monster. I startle at every rustling branch and it takes some time for me to finish my tale. When I am done, he says, "So now... you are alone here. With no savages to guard you?"

"Just the birdwoman," I say. "She comes every morning."

"Then I suppose this is the hour of our opportunity. To escape."

I lean against a tree to mull over his words. I think also of what the birdwoman has told me.

Mother, Viv, Adira, they never would have hesitated. They would have fled this abuse without second thoughts. Hell, grandmother would have done more than that. She'd have found a way to wreak vengeance on the clan for what they've done. But I'm not any of those women.

"I can't do it." I try instead to explain what the birdwoman has told me but he toots in disgust.

"You cannot trust a savage to protect you,

Miranda. You must trust in yourself, instead."

"Do you seriously think I'm capable of surviving the wilds on my own?"

At least he doesn't lie to me. Instead he says, "You are Miranda Terrasta. This life is not yours."

I shake my head. Maybe I deserve this fate, I think, for abandoning Adira. Doser can't understand.

"They killed your sisters." He's struggling to find the magic phrase that will change my mind. Somehow, deep in the core of his programming, he believes this to be a terrible idea. Or, perhaps, he longs to return to proper society. Regardless, I am moved but not swayed.

"They'll kill me, if I try to escape again. And if not them, then the monster that attacked you. I need protection. Otu, he might be—"

"If protection you want," Doser says, "then why not make the headman, or his son, the target of your *affections*? If I am to understand this society at all, and frankly I think I do *understand it*, wouldn't it be prudent to mate yourself to the most powerful man in the clan?"

I flinch at the harshness of his words; the truth he speaks is almost painful. Kono *would* be the better choice. But that, of all things, I cannot do.

I guide Doser back to the lodge and cut a strip of leather from my gown, like I see the women doing all the time when in need of a quick binding. Then I wrap it around his head, tying it tight.

"This should keep the rain off."

Across the distance we hear the first murmurings of the women beginning the day's preparations. We won't be alone long.

"I can't, Doser, I won't," I say, and this time I'm not discussing it with him, I've decided. I tried escaping and I failed. I'm done trying.

I order the robot to return to his hiding place and I forbid him from heading to Landing on his own. He floats away and despite lacking shoulders I'm sure he slumps, resigned to my decision but disagreeing with it.

I must convince Otu to take me as his wife and that is all there is to it.

With my decision made I'm desperate for my isolation to end. Desperate to return to Otu's lodge, to convince him to take me as his second wife. If anybody would've told me, when I set off from Earth, that I'd entertain such thoughts, I'd have laughed at them. Worse, I'd have scorned them up and down the Web.

"Never should have happened," I whisper to grandmother's urn more than once during the time remaining. She's my constant companion and it's easy to hold her ashes and imagine her with me, her stern face, not wrinkled like the birdwoman's, but no less wise for the absence.

I also spend many hours talking to the birdwoman, learning from her. She loves to tell me the stories and I soon come to realize that it is she that understands the words sent to her *from the heavens.* She reads what is written on the sacks of grain and incorporates them into the clan's mythology. I also learn that the headman sometimes learns to read, but Kono has never shown interest in it. In the entire clan only she and I can read, though she does not know this about me.

The days pass.

"It is time," the birdwoman says one morning.

She escorts me to the edge of town. I haven't told her about the monster in the woods, either. I suppose I am harboring a hope that it might serve me a purpose, that whatever attacked Doser might rid me of Kono. It is an impossible dream but now that I've abandoned all others, it is the only future remaining to me.

There's a cluster of men sitting around the smoldering fire in the center of the village but their backs are to me. Most of the women are out, at the secondary fire, preparing the morning meals, despite the off and on sputtering of rain. Many of them only glance at me, no nods, no greetings, their eyes dropping back to their work though I suspect they continue to watch me.

The birdwoman tugs on my arm and I lean down, towards her. Her breath is as foul as I suppose mine is but I don't cringe as she whispers into my ear.

"You have power now and some women will hate you for it."

"Power?"

"You can bear children."

And they cannot. I flush, understanding the implications. The drugs given me are gone and I'm fertile again, I'm open for business. *Jesus Christ.* Surely being capable of having children isn't going to become my superpower.

The black/orange bird nudges my finger and I stroke his tiny head a half moment; we've stopped in front of Otu's lodge. If I'm valued because I'm fertile (ick!) then I need to take advantage of that. I need to ensure that Otu takes me as a wife; I need to end my slavery.

"Especially now, the clan needs children," she says and I sense her worry. "What is *not* here? What do you not see?"

I look around. I'm used to isolating the ugly duckling on the dance floor or the out dated style or the commoner trying too hard, pretending to be of a class he's not bred for. There's only a few children and their parents and such.

"The… old. Where have—"

"All sick, like our headman. More will die." I know three elders have succumbed already, but I did not realize conditions were so grim. But she's gone before I can say more, shuffling back to her woods. She's not much for crowds, she's told me before, but I think maybe her isolation has as much to do with her needing to be outside regular society. She needs to appear *larger than life* when she is with the clan and her absences enhance her reputation, I'm sure of it.

Or is there another reason? Might she be

frightened of catching whatever illness has struck down the elderly? I can't imagine how she survives on her own, especially after what I heard in the Fen. To be alone with all those monsters. But, perhaps, there are just as many monsters here. While I linger on the empty threshold of Otu's hut, the men turn, almost as one. Their eyes fix on me, their conversation stops. I flee into the lodge.

I'm not surprised to see Zamora sitting beside Otu. Both look up, Zamora's face paler than usual as she regards me. Like the other women of the clan she knows (or believes) I'm a threat to her and though I don't want her to fear me, I can't care about that now. Not when my life is at stake.

Not knowing what to say to make her leave me alone with Otu I just glare at her. The birdwoman is right, I do have a power over the other women, because it takes a few seconds and then she rises and walks to the other side of the room, away from the hearthfire. She sits again and pretends to tidy her bed skins.

I take her place beside Otu; the folded skins they shared, warm.

"I must thank you," I say. Otu doesn't look at me, his attention focused on the flickering flames. I'm trying to use my most seductive voice but obviously the gulf between our cultures impairs his ability to understand my intent. I need be more forward and so I lean into him, our shoulders pressed together and then I grasp his hand, which he has knotted around a cord, the strands of which have colored pebbles woven into them.

My skin is still soft; his is not. It's like rubbing against asphalt.

"I *really* appreciate it," I say. I have no solid ground beneath my feet, no background experience to prepare me for this. Only the vids I've watched. I should be more patient, I know this, but I also know that patience is a luxury indulged only when time permits. And time, it does not permit.

He grunts, acknowledging my words but offering none of his own. I need to do something but still, I'm hesitant, I'm perhaps even hesitation itself, because sitting beside him has set me to trembling. I'm thinking back to the night I was captured.

You have to do this. It is grandmother's voice, speaking from the back of my mind, from the urn. She's right, of course. If I am to live, Otu has to take me.

Not Kono.

It is unimaginable that I'd ever be in this situation, on the verge of *needing* a man, instead of merely *wanting* a man. Yet I will myself to action, taking some comfort that I do not believe Otu participated in what the other men did to me after I was captured. That he alone sat away from the others. Certainly this does not make him a hero, but he is the least of all my villains.

Lunging at him with all my inexperience, my lips fumble for his. Even though he's not as tall as Kono, he is far from puny and it's like trying to climb a mountain to plant a kiss. I miss his mouth and peck his beard instead. He clenches a fist and I'm sure he's going to hit me again but then he relaxes. With more gentleness than I expect he puts his hand on my shoulder and I don't miss the quick glance he gives Zamora, who pretends not to watch us.

"Another man will take more enjoyment from you, than I."

There is a tenderness between Otu and Zamora, a bond I am growing more certain I will never breach. I envy the way he thanks her, with a pat to the hand or head, the way he invites her into his thoughts. They do not intentionally exclude me but their intimacy offers no invitation either.

I do what I can. I fill his birchbark cup with the wine that reeks like vinegar, I clean his bedding, I cut his food for him, I am watchful and attentive and as much as possible I do what needs doing before Zamora.

It soon becomes a competition. The beneficiary of our accelerated servitude is Otu and I get the impression, as the day in which I'll be sent to Kono nears, he is amused by all this.

What I can't do is share his bed. Some small part of my pride hopes that his refusal of me is an acknowledgment of his being unable to *perform* (you know 'cause he's almost old) but often enough at night I'm kept awake with his grunting as he takes his pleasure with Zamora. She is more aggressive sexually than I remember her being.

The contest is hers.

Grandmother's urn has no answers for me though I still spend my scarce idle moments rubbing it; failed attempts to conjure her wisdom. Four more old timers die and the village is never quiet; there is always some poor family wailing. And Otu spends hours each day guiding the hunters because Kono seldom leaves his sick father's lodge.

"Will he die?" I ask Zamora one afternoon. The two of us are carrying buckets of water from a nearby stream back to the village. The waterway carves its way down a hill of crumbling stone, through the foothills leading to the mountains that surround us (or as I think of them, my prison walls). Having conceded our contest for Otu I decide I should try instead, to win her friendship.

(If I survive my time with Kono I will need a friend.)

"Don't ever say that." She explains that we must not speak of the headman's death, that we must pretend it is not possible. It is blasphemy to presume him mortal. But how am I to avoid these thoughts? The merciless wind spews the pyre smoke back towards the village every day. It does not bother the savages because they consider the smoke a soulspirit and it is a comfort to them. To me it is a disgusting and constant reminder of death.

Yet as we near the village a squeal of dismay from the headman's lodge startles us. Zamora turns her head, meeting my gaze, and I wonder if she thinks that somehow my words have slain the old man.

The hide parts swiftly and Kono's first wife stumbles out, her lip bleeding. She's been beaten again, Kono's rage is at its apex; his grief has brought with it irrationality and destructiveness. Otu complains about this daily, a proper headman, he says, must always be calm and rational.

"The illness is tearing them apart," Zamora says, dispassionately, reminding me again that she is not from this clan. I've tried talking to her about her past but she says little.

I have no reply. I stare after the bloodied woman. This is to be my fate. Soon I'll belong to Kono.

Except, maybe there is another way.

I remember growing up, how my sisters would tease me, that I never paid attention to anything at all. I never mastered economics or science; history or programming. How I hated their teasing but when I tried to explain the latest fashion trend to them or why I thought a guy/gal or a gal/gal or a guy/guy had hooked up, they ignored me. They scorned me when I recommended bands or showed off the moves to a new dance. They failed to see the value in any of that.

But the *watching*, it was important. And, in my defeat, it is all that is left to me. To watch. Not long before I'm sent to what will assuredly be a living hell, I'm listening to my roommates, who remain inside, while I scrape food from our bowls into the compost.

"My influence will fade," Otu says and there's a palpable fear in his voice. Kono has his own companions, his own advisers and I'm starting to suspect that there will be no room for Otu in the new headman's court. I peer into the lodge, watching them, without trying to be obvious that I'm doing so.

"We'll survive," Zamora says, her gaze directed towards the floorboards as she leans against him.

Otu snorts. "Kono is too rash, doesn't plan as his father would. We have so many sick. Last night Jaks died and I worry his son has not yet learned all his father had to teach him. The clan will suffer for it."

"Many sons *seem to* lack what their fathers had but Jaks was old. It was not unexpected."

"Yet almost all our elders are sick and most shall die," he says. "Their soulspirits will fly away with all their lessons and stories, all that they might teach the young. Moons ago I warned Kono to separate the old that were not yet sick from the others but he refused. Now they are all dying. But they don't blame Kono. They blame me."

I stare at the empty bowls in my hand.

"Because of her," Zamora says. I am almost

185

always *her* or *she* to them.

"Yes," he says and I can't listen anymore.

"What have I done?" I demand, as I step into the lodge.

Zamora cringes, at my boldness, but Otu ignores the offense. They rise, as one.

"They believe you brought the sickness to us," he says, "as punishment for what was done to you."

I'm stunned. If I had such power then why would I endure the indignities they make me suffer? What foolishness, what fools!

"Do you *believe* that?"

"If Otu did, he would have strangled you himself," Zamora says but it's hardly an answer.

He has not thrown me out, but he has not welcomed me either. Is this why he won't touch me? Is he afraid of using me the way the other men have? Or does his concern for the clan override his immediate needs? Is his worry somehow key?

"I can help, I think." It is maybe a half truth but still truthful enough. Zamora shakes her head and tells me there is no help, that the sickness will move from man to man, from woman to woman, until the clan is no more, but Otu, he is not so willing to abandon hope and he strides to me, commands me to speak. His face is serious and I know that if I do not answer him well I will suffer for it.

"I know how to breach the Tower."

He grasps his necklace and pales.

"That is forbidden."

"Inside it are medicines of all kinds."

Otu releases his talisman. "A cure, for this sickness?"

Here I know I'm more lying than guessing but I nod anyways. There is always the *possibility* that Landing's medical facility might have what they need.

"If this is true," he murmurs, "Kono might send men there. Convincing him though, won't be easy. And then he'll have to find us a way across the waters."

I smile. "I already know a way. A secret way."

Otu opens his mouth to reply but Zamora interjects, "And Kono, he does not need to learn of this, my husband."

I understand her intent immediately. The Tower might give Otu the leverage he needs to stay relevant, to ensure he has a role in the clan's future, after the headman dies. I've underestimated her; she's thinking of longterm survival. Just like me.

Otu regards his wife with pride. "I'll lead a small party and tell Kono we intend to hunt in the forest. It is not an unusual request, for the deer are more plentiful outside our valley." Otu's eyes are bright and intense as he speaks. "And there's also a giant, near the bay. We have many reasons to make the expedition."

"And you need me to guide you, to reach the Tower."

He clucks his tongue, almost smiles.

"On a long hunt it is not uncommon for a

slave to accompany the men, to take care of their *needs*."

I struggle to remain composed, to ignore what he suggests. This is the tricky part but if Otu has half the brains I pray he does, I'm sure he's expecting it. My heart beats hard, my palms sweat. "It would not be proper, Otu, for a mere *slave* to accompany you." I flush, wringing my hands together. I wish that Zamora and I were friends, that she might support me in this. But it falls to me, alone, to be bold. "There is only one man whose needs I wish to attend to."

He raises an eyebrow.

"This… this woman, would prefer to accompany her *husband*, on such a trek."

"I already have a wife," Otu says before Zamora protests my suggestion.

I shrug, pretending defeat. I have watched the women of this clan long enough to know that even with their limited power they still exert influence.

"You do. But… but a man who is bold enough to lead his clan in such troubling times, such a man should have many wives, should he not?"

CHAPTER 17

The Woman Who is Always Wrong

Salva will never learn of this.

Not just that Otu will take me as his wife tomorrow in a ceremony that will make him my protector and my provider. Salva must also never learn that I'm not entirely unhappy about the situation.

Sure, I'd rather be home, maybe even waking in Salva's arms, and not those of this savage, but this morning, it is the first that I wake without fear, since my isolation. Zamora sleeps on Otu's other side, our man wedged between us. Before the others wake I clean myself and stoke the hearthfire, starting the water boiling for the ground grains that will be breakfast.

I've done it. I've saved myself.

"Satisfied, sister?"

I startle, almost dropping the wooden ladle. Zamora has wrapped her skins tight around herself to join me by the fire. She's looking at me in a odd way.

Feeling defensive, I say, "I do not want to come between you—"

"You won't. You are merely a tool, for him, for us." Otu's snores mask the patter of raindrops on the roof.

I shrug. I must not be angry with her. If I were in her place, I would be as she is, but why can't she understand that it's better for us, for all three of us, to be allies?

I try to bridge the gulf between us. "It can't be Kono." *Again.* "I want to survive. Like you."

After Otu wakes we eat and scheme. Once the marriage is official Otu will lobby for a hunting expedition. He explains, as he shovels spoonful after spoonful of gruel into his mouth (much of it ending up in his beard) that most of the hunters will understand his desire to leave, that a first wife is often jealous, that a man who takes a second prefers to spend his time alone with the new wife without interference from the first. The marriage itself helps to provide the cover we need to travel to the Tower.

He (and I) watch Zamora throughout this part of the conversation, but her face stays blank, as if unaffected. And maybe she is. She's learned to survive and she knows, that in this situation, there's little chance of Otu's affection transferring to me. That I am, as she said, a tool.

Our success, seems inevitable until the day that wild shrieking pervades the village.

Otu rushes from the lodge with his spear and Zamora and I position ourself at our doorway to stare at the commons. The entire village mills in front of the headman's lodge, with the women and men side by side, all kneeling and tearing at their clothing. The children are wailing too, though I suspect that's because their parents are freaking the shit out of them.

"Oh no," Zamora whispers. Otu buries his spear into the ground and reaches the entrance to the headman's hut as Kono emerges. The younger man carries his father in his arms, trailed by Kono's wives.

The headman is dead.

Kono is the new headman.

It is as if my mere acknowledgment of this angers Kono and he swivels his head, his beard brushing his father's corpse as he stares over the heads of the mourners.

"You," Kono says. I clutch the wall for support. There's no storm, only a light rainfall, but for me it is as if the day has become a night filled with arcs of lightning and a terrible thunder descending over me, a blinding, deafening cacophony of light and sound.

Kono strides towards me, the crowd parting for him. They watch his disruption of their bereavement with confusion and fear. The smell of funereal smoke lingers in the air. Customarily the clan burns their dead to release the soulspirits but they usually wait three days before doing so to allow the family time to honor the corpse. But the fear of sickness has waived this waiting period and now the corpses are immediately consigned to the flames, to prevent the spread of contagion.

"Nidawi's witch, she has brought this upon us," he says. "She must be thrown onto the pyre with my father."

I almost bolt. There's no way I'm going to be burnt alive. But I don't have to flee because Otu plants his hand firm on Kono's shoulder and whispers to the younger man. Kono brushes Otu away, drawing his father close to his chest, his muscles trembling with the sustained effort.

"I tire of your weakness, Otu. Our magician has vanished, her life likely stolen by this slave. Too many have died and their deaths, all of them, are on her hands. And on yours, if you continue to protect her."

"I am not—"

"She has seduced you, Otu. She has tricked you into naming her as wife. Deceived my father's *wisest* adviser."

Otu steps back but when Kono barks at the hunters to grab my arms, to drag me to the pyre, he speaks again. This time Otu addresses the clan, not Kono.

"We do not kill, not when we mourn a fallen headman. Do not forget your father's customs!"

It is Kono who keeps himself silent this

192

time, for the clan's beliefs are terribly important to the people. Frustrated, he turns and marches, stiff-legged, towards the pyres. I release my breath as the parade of mourners follow him. Zamora joins them but she advises me to stay, lest I cause further disturbance. I am in total agreement.

(And I do not flee, when I might have, because I still believe I have succeeded, that Otu will make me his wife. It seems, that my destiny on Terrasta is to be the Woman Who Is Always Wrong.)

No hunting or killing is permitted during the mourning period. This is what Otu says. But no marriages are allowed either.

I am still a *slave* and not a wife, I will be sent to Kono's lodge, as per the original arrangement. The dead headman has flown away with all my plans. There is no safe haven from the smell of charred corpses. Even Kal's head has been thrown into the flames. And here, on my last day of freedom, I sit and wait.

Kono will take his vengeance on me, will hurt me for every slight he imagines I have inflicted on the clan. My guts are tight, coiled. For no reason I might imagine, last night, Otu took me to his bed with a fury I never expected of him. Our plans, for the Tower, are on hold.

He insists they are not forgotten.

I do not have to serve an entire month with Kono. Only fifteen days, the length of mourning remaining. After that I might still be Otu's wife.

If I survive.

"You hair is a mess," Zamora says, settling in beside me. Otu is out, at the corpse fires but the women have returned to prepare the afternoon meals.

I don't know if Zamora is pleased that I'm leaving Otu's lodge but she hasn't acted like she is. She's actually been somewhat nicer than usual. She reaches for my hair, to braid it in imitation of her own, though mine is too short to do much with now. I don't particularly want to be pretty for Kono, but I'm frightened enough for my future that any attention from a friend, is welcome.

"I don't know if I can do this," I say, some time later, my braid half woven. We've chatted, but about everything else and not the horrible fate hanging over my head.

Today I belong to Kono.

Zamora twists my hair, tightening the coils. "There is a way out." She's behind me and I can't see her face, can't see if she's serious and sensitive, or cruel and mocking.

"There's nothing."

"You might do what your sister did."

"What do you know of Adira??" I cry, spinning, undoing her work.

"Adira? A pretty name, I didn't know it, but Otu… he told me what the girl… Adira… what she did."

What she did.

"They... Kono killed her. I saw... saw her burnt. Sacrificed."

"No, Miranda. She threw herself from a cliff, rather than...."

The truth hits me, as if Zamora slaps me across the face with it. My sister killed herself to avoid abuse, and this is what Zamora is suggesting I might do. But I'm not as brave as it appears Adira has been.

"I can't do that."

"Then you have no choice but to bear this." She has not been kind but she's offered me more than anybody else here has. She's told me what happened to Adira. We hear voices as the men return.

"I suppose it is now time," I say.

"Your braids, I could finish them, first."

I shake my head. "What would be the point?" I take up grandmother's urn and hand it to Zamora. They'll be safer here. Then I cross the damp commons to Kono's home and place myself once more under the Savage's power.

I don't remember.

I'm a nobody, a nothing, invisible, unremembered.

Unremarkable.

Just a shell.

Except a shell that must wake. Kono's wives, the elder, Mara, and the younger, Lann, prod me with words and toes and I roll from my hides.

Waking brings remembering.

A quick glance confirms Kono still sleeps. I won't survive long enough for the mourning period to end.

We do not live in the headman's lodge, no man or woman may set foot inside it until the mourning is finished. Instead we are inside Kono's own lodge and it is a poor home, for he has spent too much time under his father's roof.

There are gaps in the logs, where wind and rain have taken their toll on the mud used to fill in the spaces between them. Enough light filters in through the gaps to tell me it is still dark outside, the earliest part of morning. I am not surprised when Mara and Lann return to their bedding, leaving me to stir the embers and replenish the hearth.

Three mornings. Four *nights*.

I won't survive. And if I do, I must… forget. Whomever this woman is that I've become, she must be buried, she must be destroyed. Drugs enough back on Earth to make that happen and now, after a few days under Kono's hand, I am more committed to that path, to destroying all evidence of who I am. To forgetting.

"Back to work," I murmur to grandmother, though she cannot hear me 'cause she's not under the same roof as I.

I start preparing breakfast. I use a thin-bladed knife to cut tough strips of meat into manageable pieces. These will supplement the boiling grains. The knife's metal is dull brown and its handle is wrapped with thin strips of leather. It is not unlike the other knives I've used in other lodges, except perhaps of finer material.

When I look up Kono is sitting across from me. Or maybe not sitting, a man like Kono never actually *just sits*. He leans towards me, on his knees, towering, as usual.

"You are clumsy and slow," he says and I nod, in agreement, staring at the knife's blade. There is no denying it, I am less skilled than his other wives.

If there is any sliver of redemption in Kono's it is that he genuinely mourns his father. His beard and hair are unkempt, his skin sallow, great bags under his eyes. But for all that I feel no pity for the man, for the bastard he mourns was as savage, as cold, as the monster before me. Neither are worthy of tear or remembrance.

"You have many things to learn," he says, as if he's narrating my life's faults.

"I'm trying."

He snorts and he tries on a smile, as if to pretend amusement in front of me, as if to pretend that I'm amusing, or so far beneath him, that I'm only worthy of jest.

"Otu tells me that the other woman we captured was your sister," he says and I nod. "But what Otu does not know, what none of us know, is why she traveled with that Birdeater."

With Kal.

I do not know if he is asking me a question, so I don't say anything, my hands moving towards the bowls full of boiled water, ready to stir in the grains.

He grasps my wrist, spilling the grain.

"Why was she, and you, with Kal?" he asks.

He must know the answer to it, already! But his pressure does not diminish and I'm forced to tell him that Kal was escorting us to the Birdeater's clan.

Kono releases me and scratches at his beard, his heavy shoulders slanted forward as if to remind me how much potent power remains within him.

"You are the Birdeater's ally!" It is an accusation and I almost tease him with it, but I'm too frightened to do so. Too frightened to play games with this man's mind.

"You must know," I say, instead, "you shot our shuttle from the sky. You attacked us at...."

I stop, sudden realization slamming into me. After all our conversations, I'm sure Otu has never been to the Tower. That — and Kono's words now — surely means this clan was not behind the attack. But if not they, then who?

I clamp my mouth shut and cut more of the meat. Kono rises and turns his back to me, his shoulders squared and rigid. "He was a headman's son, like me."

I hesitate in the cutting and if I were truly my mother's daughter I'd have thrust the knife into his chest.

He was nothing like you.

"Kal?"

"They Promoted him, instead of a man of our clan," he says, turning on me, his eyes angry and violent as he stabs his finger towards the sky. "Why did they take him? Are we not worthy? Am I *not* worthy!"

There are actual tears in his eyes and I'm stunned. Gehum has fabricated such a convincing illusion. He is devastated and jealous that he was not taken. Kono lunges and drags me to my feet.

"I killed him though, didn't I?" Kono says, "they thought him worthy and he was not."

"He was—"

Kono strikes me, a backhand blow across my face that would have sent me flying across the room except he holds my arm tight. He's smiling but there's no joy in his eyes, it is a fabrication, to keep me frightened, I think. And it is working. I am frightened.

"The Birdeater almost made it; we were tracking men from his clan not far from where we found you. Planned to ambush the dogs." I'm fully confused now because I'm sure Kal did not think his clan quite so near. "But then your... vessel fell and Kal was there, and it was a sign, wasn't it? The godlings delivering to us the son of our enemy."

"You attacked us; we didn't *fall*." I know it's stupid of me to argue with him but there's certain parts of me that don't shut up and listen, even when I'm screaming at them to do so. His eyes narrow and I cringe, preparing myself for another slap.

"When a man kills another, he absorbs the power of the conquered," Kono says, "as I have done with Kal Rothson. All that was his, is now mine. Now I am worthy."

He stares at me and I realize he's pieced together things, or thinks he has. I was in the shuttle with Kal and maybe he's even thinking that I select the Promoted.

"I do not choose," I say. I have no power and I see that he *sees* this, when the bright fire of madness dims in his eyes. His voice becomes low and utterly terrifying.

"Look down!" He barks and I obey, trembling as he mutters on about a woman's place, her duty to please the men of the clan. "*That*, especially, you must learn. Otu is lazy, weak, but in my lodge, you will learn."

"I do my best," I give him those words, instead of the stabbing he deserves.

"Your sister was no good either," he says, grasping my hair. Tears flood my eyes at the jolt of pain. "She was cold and lifeless beneath us, like a fish. That's why we killed her."

He jerks my head up and down, forcing me to nod, to agree with him, but I'm not agreeing, not in the least. Adira killed herself. Though Zamora might lie to me as easily as Kono I trust in the sincerity of her words more than in his. He never killed my sister. Kono is a liar and a man only lies, grandmother used to say, when he wants something or is hiding something.

Which is it, Kono?

Chapter 18

Marriage Box

The day the period of mourning ends, I wake earlier than the others, as the first feeble rays of morning sun trickle through the wall gaps. It has only been two weeks yet I have never known such exhaustion. The ordeal I suffered before was momentarily (no less horrific for it) but this has been day after day of not knowing who will strike me next, how I will be abused. If not for what has come before, I do not think I'd have survived it.

"But, grandmother," I whisper, across the commons, to her ashes, "I am more clever than before, am I not?" I've learned to hide myself inside my own mind. Let them treat the body as they wish. One day the real Miranda will return to it and she'll never have to think again of this time. It shall be forgotten.

I do not know the protocol so I continue

with the morning meal, as usual, and take the scolding from Kono's wives when they wake. When Kono rises he kicks me in the side and tells me the gruel tastes *worse than shit*. (Like, really, how would he know that, right?)

Yet the wives smile and joke with each other. Their headman has been honored and it is time for the mourning to end.

I serve, not knowing how to ask the question, how to ask *may I leave now?* I have not really spoken to Otu or Zamora or anybody else since my time with Kono began. The sun warms the commons outside and there are footfalls and the soft voices of sombre children and their parents. Outside the clan assembles. Tonight they greet their new headman.

I watch Mara and Lann enact an almost startling transformation. Kono's hair and beard are trimmed with the same knife I use in the kitchen. They boil water and sponge him. Then they braid his hair and beard with slivers of colored metal and painted bone.

Through their magic Kono becomes the headman. Afterwards they clean and dress themselves, occasionally ordering me to fetch this or that and I obey, not knowing if I should be preparing myself, not daring to ask.

Then, after the day passes, the celebration begins and they leave me alone in the lodge, swept up in celebration. I watch from the doorway as the men and women dance and sing and eat. Zamora and Otu join the others, smiling and clapping their hands as they welcome Kono as their new leader.

Neither glances at me, not even once. I'm starting to wonder if I'm to be a sacrifice. I nibble food from the pantry, but mostly I watch and wait. The ceremony seems comprised of speeches by the men. They all honor Kono's bravery and intelligence.

"They sure kiss their king's ass, don't they?" I whisper to grandmother. She has a special hate reserved for the few lingering remnants of monarchies left in our world, primitive tokens of that perverse period the human race had forced themselves through, when merit alone was not sufficient to be successful.

The hours drag on as the orators seek to outdo one another for verbosity. I struggle to stay awake and soon focus on the hissing and spitting of the torches and the bonfire instead of the droning speeches.

It is a struggle to stay awake.

Until the birdwoman returns.

I hear gasps from the fringes of the audience and my eyes pop open (here's me not realizing I've closed them). The gasps fade with a swiftness that is unnerving and then I see her, coming in from the opposite side of the village, the crowd parting as if to avoid her.

The clan's magician carries a wooden box.

I step away from Kono's lodge, moved as much by concern as curiosity. The birdwoman looks terrible. Her hair hangs limp over her shoulders and her eyes seem spongy and puffy, even in the torchlight. She's sick, or has been sick, and without her coat of birds she'd be little more than a shambling skeleton.

She approaches Kono, who sits at the head of his feast table. Higher prestige families, comprised mostly of Kono's new advisers, sit near the headman. Otu and Zamora are about midways down the table.

Kono does not rise and by the crowd's nervous chattering I wonder if he should have.

The birdwoman sets her box on the table and Kono glances at it, his eyebrows rising. She says more to him and his face darkens beneath the flickering flames. He rises, finally, stepping to the side of the birdwoman, his head bowed in thought as she stands where he has been sitting.

There's a canopy of stars behind her, a backdrop of velvet studded with gold and complemented by a full moon. The long torch shafts spaced along the feasting table mingle the celestial light with terrestrial flame and their combined might casts long shadows. Despite her illness, the birdwoman has a presence that dwarfs even Kono in his splendid robes.

"We are the blessed!" Her voice is different and unlike what her frame suggests possible. There's a murmur, a word the crowd says, that I don't quite make out. "We are the blessed, the chosen, of those who survived Nidawi's wrath. We, the blessed, alone, follow godlings's way. In their wisdom they have taken Bly Ryikson and have *honored* us with his son, Kono Blyson. A strong hunter, a powerful warrior."

She pauses and there's a cheer that stops the moment she resumes.

"In time, may the godlings grant Kono Blyson his father's wisdom and his father's faith. Then, he too, will have the true counsel of the godlings and be counted among the blessed."

Then the birdwoman smiles and raises the box from the table. "And as his first act as headman, Kono Blyson, will perform a marriage ceremony, tonight, beneath the Orphan's gaze."

The clan rises in confused delight but the birdwoman stares past them. Stares at me. The box she holds is for me. My marriage box.

"It is beautiful," Zamora says. She's braiding my hair and this time I'm letting her finish it. This time I have something to look forward to. And really, had anybody suggested that I might anticipate marrying an unfashionable savage just a couple pegs above knuckle dragging Neanderthal, I'd have snarked them out.

I glance at the box which I've placed on Otu's floor, in front of where I'm sitting cross-legged. Zamora is behind me, her calloused fingers working my hair with vigor. With all the hair pulling Kono's inflicted on me, it hurts, but I'm past caring. The worst is behind me. I've leveraged the situation so that I'm no longer in harm's way and now either I'll be rescued or Otu will bring me to safety. It might take weeks or months but I'll fly home and banish this nightmare.

"And I can't open it?"

I am curious, maybe tormented by, the thought of what the birdwoman might have placed inside it, for me. By building my marriage box she has taken me into her family and were she not a savage I'd be grateful. She has marked me as being important and even now, before the marriage ceremony, I am no longer a slave. I've seen it in the men's eyes, in the women's, as Zamora escorted me back to Otu's lodge.

Outside, my future *husband* and his clan wait for me. Though they are exhausted they are also excited and there will be no delaying the ceremony the birdwoman has maneuvered Kono into performing. She is clever.

"Not until the morning after your first night together," Zamora answers and there's a quality in her voice I can't quite identify. Jealousy? Likely. But also curiosity too, I think.

If this is a common ground between us, I need to take advantage of it. We will be living together and I want (no, I need!) a friend. I miss having a confidante. I want to talk to somebody, to gossip. I'd love to even be silly, but I accept that as being impossible until my rescue.

(God, I can't remember what being silly feels like. Dancing and yacking and flirting. Jesus Christ, this world sucks.)

"What do you think is inside?"

"Your past and your future," she says.

"What does that mean?"

"You and I have no mothers, here." Zamora's staring down at me (and if it were me saying her words I'm sure I'd have started misting up right there and then) but she is a Zamora and not a Miranda. "But your *new* mother packed it with items that have meaning from before your marriage to remind you of what you were, of where you came from."

That part makes sense. "But she can't know the future."

Zamora says, "It is not prediction, it is hope. Our mothers pack their hopes for our futures in the boxes."

I mull on that as Zamora finishes braiding. I admit it, I'm growing apprehensive, not about what is inside the box, but at the prospect of marriage, of marrying, of being a wife. I'm losing track of time but it seems not so long ago that I was perfectly single but on a trajectory to marry the most powerful man in the universe. Not a middle-aged savage.

Still, I tremble as Zamora pronounces her work complete. I stand, my fingers touching the braids.

"Wish I might see it," I say. There are no mirrors here and other than glimpsing my reflection in the stream, I haven't seen *myself* in a long while.

Zamora's face twists up as if I've stomped on her foot. "I've done as fine work as is possible considering the length."

I've offended her! I'm quick to apologize. "It is just, where I'm from, we have…." and here I engage her for several minutes, trying to explain what a mirror is. I believe she grasps the mechanics well enough but her mind is incapable of grasping *why* I'd want a mirror.

"To see myself."

"But… what point is there, in that?"

"To make myself beautiful." This seems a rather poor answer, so I elaborate. "To make *sure* I'm beautiful, I guess."

"Why not ask another? Why trust a… thing?"

I shrug. "A friend might lie, maybe. To protect my feelings."

Her eyes narrow. This too is an insufficient answer.

"Sometimes, there's nobody around. A mirror lets you do it yourself. On your own."

Zamora shakes her head. "Here, with the clan, you must learn to trust, Miranda. We only have one another. We need no mirrors."

She whirls away. This is impossible. I am impossible. Somehow I've well and truly offended her. But there's no time to make amends, not now.

Compared with the magnificence of the headman ceremony, my marriage to Otu is rushed. But I do not care. I want it over. I want to know that Kono will never claw at me again, never press himself against me. Never have power over me.

The headman asks the godlings for their blessing and the birdwoman assures him they are given and then Kono wraps a leather cord around Otu's hand and mine, binding us and we sup well and late into the night, the children falling asleep on the ground, adults joining them there later. The weather holds.

I have never had trouble sleeping, not in the entirety of my life, but after the ceremony, after the eating and the drinking and the consummation of our marriage, I still cannot sleep. I should, I know, for I have succeeded. I will be protected.

Perhaps *that* itself is the reason I don't sleep. For what Terrastan gal has ever needed the protection of a man? What sort of civilization makes that a necessity? Nobody else seems to have trouble sleeping, Otu's chest rises and falls; he snores but not excessively. Zamora is quieter in her sleep, on the other side of the lodge, in my customary spot.

I miss my meds. I miss taking them, and I suspect, I am failing to find the sleep I desire due, in large part, to their being missing. Without the medication I'm merely human.

"Kono will lead us to ruin."

I blink, turning towards Otu. He's sitting up and I think he's having a nightmare, talking in his sleep, but then I notice the first streaks of morning's light through the doorway.

"He is a cruel man." I say, starting to rise, to stoke the hearthfire, but Otu places his hand on

209

my wrist, gently, but with some pressure, and I am reminded of last night, with him, and I flush.

I should not care to be touched by him. I should not want to be touched by him. Yet somehow, last night, was different, and that's the last thing in all the world I want.

"Cruel, yes. But worse, he's reckless. He risked our lives, tracking the Birdeaters, last spring. An unnecessary waste that ate away our days; days better spent hunting. Kono has tasted the fight, the kill. He enjoys it too much."

"You do not?"

Otu shrugs. "A raid here and there, for women," he says, glancing at his first wife, "that is our way. But Kono thinks differently. He talks of… I have no real words for it."

"War," I say, "he makes war against them. Fighting, never ending."

"Yes, war. That is right. And for Kono there will always be another war."

I wet my lips, thinking back to my conversation with Kono, his obliviousness to the tragedy that granted me the cruel fate I now suffer. Needing to *know*, I attempt to learn from Otu what I could not from Kono.

"Is that why he shot us down?"

Otu's stare is as blank as polished river stone and it takes me several minutes to explain to him what happened to our shuttle (and what a shuttle even is!). By the time I finish my explanation, I know I was right earlier. Kono's clan was not responsible for our shuttle's crash.

But Otu does not leave me time to think that over much because my talk of flying machines and rockets and star jaunts, brings a gleam to his eyes. He becomes animated, his entire body rocking, like an unmedicated child. He presses me for details about my world (which I give; screw the protocol about not letting the savages learn too much). He is especially keen to understand the Tower's wonders.

"I've often dreamed," he says, "of what might be inside it. Some believe it to be the home of Tyee, the True Magician. That is why, they say, that it is covered, year round, by thousands of birds. That is why, we are told to avoid it, else we interfere with the godlings's world."

There's a warning in his words, and I nod. I get it. Don't talk about the Tower to anybody else.

"It will be yours," I say. I've watched and I've learned and though Otu is a gentler savage, he is still a savage. He wants to be headman. In this there is little difference between the men of Terrasta and men of Earth. Power flows more swiftly through their veins than blood.

"Summer brings strong storms and we'll use that to our advantage. We'll pretend to be lost, delayed. It will give us the time we need."

I smile but then his grip tightens. "You have not lied, to me?"

"I have not," I whisper.

His grip loosens and he stares away from

me, Zamora, the lodge, even the village itself, I think. He's staring into the future and for the first time I'm actually frightened of him. He rises and dresses, waking Zamora to talk this through with her.

(I'll never take her place, in his heart, but I'm okay with that.)

The marriage box is still waiting for me and, remembering Zamora's words from last night, I open it. I almost expect it to be empty, because really, what can the birdwoman know about me, but when I raise the lid I must bite my lip to keep from gasping. Inside the small chest are two items.

One is from my past and one is for my future but right then, I can't say which is which: the electronic tablet that contains my mother's journal or Mr. Decker's revolver.

CHAPTER 19

The Birdwoman's Altar

Summer as a child was always a wonderful time but now, as an adult, it is a disappointment. Maybe this is a universal truth. I think shit like this too much now, my brain no longer protected and insulated by medication. But today, I try more than usual, to enjoy it.

The afternoon sun is bright and brilliant. Zamora, myself, and a handful of other women are working on the side of a rocky cliff face, south of the village. We accompanied the hunters here but after they killed several mountain goats, they've returned to the village, leaving the butchering to the women.

Almost a month has passed since my rushed marriage and though rains and ceremonies have kept Otu from following through with our plan, my situation has still improved, drastically. The vegetation is in full summer bloom and the clan lacks for little but the greatest change is in the way the clan looks at me, talks to me. I've become accepted, and only Kono's wives, and the headman himself, keep their distance.

(Whether to avoid me or not, Kono and his family did not accompany the hunters on this hunt.)

The women sing as they work and if not for the gruesome task at hand, it might have been beautiful. Often I look up and see them smiling and I smile back at them. Such joy! Even with their arms covered in blood.

Though I avoid the bloodiest of the work (mostly fetching things for the other women) I try my best to fit in. I have learned the names of the children and their parents and their lineages. I am learning which herbs to collect when we walk the valleys that surround the village, I am learning how to cook more than gruel; I am becoming Otu's woman.

I fill a birchbark cup with water from a leather flask and hand it to Zamora. She's just finished scraping the hide from the last of the goats. I avoid looking at the animal's heads (for all seem to stare at me) and focus instead on Zamora. I am trying to win her friendship but it is difficult because Otu often shares his bed with me.

(What Zamora does not know is that most nights we simply talk; our conspiring whispers slipping away with the curling smoke of the hearthfire. Rarely does he make use of me. And the only gift he has given me was when he returned my boots.)

She thanks me and sips the water. Her eyes do not stray from my face but she should not worry. This is not my first kill site; I've lost the urge to vomit at the butchered, reeking, corpses. I don't like it any but I know we have to eat and it seems that on Terrasta summers are brief; the hunters are busy replenishing our supplies of meat, meat that will be dried and preserved to last us through what, if the clan speaks truth, will be a prolonged and frigid winter.

(With real snow and everything.)

She sets the cup down, turning back to her work and I sigh, another lost moment between us. No matter what I try, I cannot build this friendship between us. The morning after opening my marriage box I showed her the revolver and the journal but she merely shrugged and moved on with her day. Now she gestures to where two of the women are starting to roll chunks of meat inside the hides.

"Go on, help them," she says and I join the singing women (though I don't sing myself, because we all know I haven't the voice). I help them roll the hides tight over their bundles, and tie them with woven cord.

"How will we bring these back?"

A woman humors me with a smile. "We carry them."

My eyes must have grown wide at that

because everyone giggles. The women take their only break as the sun starts to wane and the last of the meat is ready for transport. They cluster around Zamora, chatting while I stand on their fringes.

A rustling in the sparse trees growing on the slope below me draws me away from the others. I do not walk too far, I am not foolish, I know what the others do not. There is a monster in our valley. But this is not what is making the noise now.

Doser's blue eye is barely visible beneath the boughs of a pine tree. The robot and I speak seldom now; he's displeased that I won't flee with him, displeased at the plan I have concocted with Otu. But it is a comfort to know that he often trails me when I leave the village, keeping an eye out for me. I give him a slight wave and a smile.

"Have you found something?"

I spin and find Zamora standing right behind me and when I tell her no her cheeks flush and she steps past me, staring into the brush.

"Was it an animal?" I duck my head to avoid eye contact when I lie and tell her that it was a squirrel. The robot is my last secret and she can't learn of him. She orders me back to work and I obey, though I'm dismayed. I've lost another opportunity to build our friendship.

Zamora is no fool. She knows I'm hiding something from her.

Despite my earlier judgment the weight, while sufficient to bend my knees, is not unbearable and soon we march down the stone littered path, moving with the sureness of the dead goats on our backs, as if we've inherited their sure footedness.

Zamora leads the way and I scramble to keep close to her. The other women stay just behind us. Nobody is ever really alone in the clan, which I find strange, this idea of everything being done in a group, as if we were all online together, but listening to their conversation reminds me of what I've lost.

My preference is (and always will be) to have the choice of when to invite others into my life, but I am envious of the ease in which the women's conversation flows while they march. If a woman missteps, there's an instinctive quiet as she adjusts her load before conversation resumes. It is as if they are all of one mind.

While I admire their camaraderie I see the weakness they are blind to. They are too simple to realize that their groupthink makes it easy for a strong and cruel man like Kono to be their dictator. They are too accustomed to obeying orders.

Between Zamora and myself, there's only silence. With another girlfriend I might have joked about our relationships, but given that Zamora and I share the same man, that is hardly healthy. Finally, I grow desperate.

"Do you ever miss your family?"

She does not reply.

"I do. Even my mother."

She glances over her shoulder and I think she's trying not to smile. Taking this as a victory I start rattling on, telling her all about Adira and Viv and mother. Then I try to explain to her the twins and she almost stops, right there on the trail.

"A brother and sister, born at the same time?" she asks, slowing her pace so that I don't have to hurry quite so much to keep up with her.

"Yes, twins, they are—"

"A blessing, a sign that the godlings favor the family. They were common in my family," she says, going on to tell me about her aunts, and several others, in her clan who were twins. "My brothers were twins too. I think I miss them the most."

Twins and brothers! Now I've found common ground with her. If I weren't carrying half a goat I think I might have bounced with joy.

"What were they like?"

"Very different, from one another. Errik, is serious, as if being a few minutes older than Kal has—"

"Kal's your brother?!" I blurt it out.

"Yes." She stops us in the middle of the trail, which isn't as awkward as it sounds given that we've distanced ourselves rather considerably from the other women. "Were you really with him? You and your sister? Otu refuses to talk much about what happened that day."

218

I am almost stunned. I knew that Zamora was from the same clan as Kal but did not realize they were related. That they were brother and sister.

"I did know him, briefly. I… liked him." The last I don't say to please her, I say it because it is a truth.

"He might have been headman; he was father's favorite. Now I imagine Errik has taken the duty, instead."

I nod, not certain what to say next, stumbling over the words I need to kindle this friendship. "It… must have been an honor when Kal was chosen."

"It was, though he was not the first of our family. Our uncle was also Promoted, two festivals before Kal. That was many, many years ago. Kal really looked up to him and followed him everywhere, even though when he came back, uncle changed. He used to be loud and generous but returned a quieter man. Your world is terrible; it breaks men."

I remember Kal's conversation, how it unnerved him the importance of women in Earth society. I wonder if he was returning changed too.

"It was never terrible to me. But it is different. The differences, I suppose, must be hard for newcomers."

She nods and I think we are done talking about this but a moment later I wish we were, because Zamora asks the one question she should not.

"Did Kal die, horribly?"

We stare at each other, she with her hair lightened by the sun, so that it is almost white, her eyes pale blue; the women of the clan are exotic, I think, compared with us, the Distinguished. They are rare gemstones. She's harder than I, stronger, and I decide the truth won't break her.

"Yes," I say. She doesn't need the details, just a name, I think, and I give her it. "Kono."

She nods again, then turns away to resume our walk.

After a hasty meal, Otu escorts Zamora and I from our lodge. Despite our exhaustion and the lateness of the hour, he's eager and we do not refuse him. We both carry torches but Otu's burden is a haunch of goat meat, wrapped in hide. An offering, he has said.

"I don't like this place," Zamora says, when we arrive at the boneyard. My legs are screaming in protest, for we've ascended a trail of loose shale, to reach this location.

"You're telling me." Even though it is difficult to see much, the grotto is a place of nightmares, filled as it is by bones. And these are not normal bones, not the thin leg bones of goats, not the tapered skulls of forest deer. These bones are thick and robust, with ridged skulls whose empty eye holes glare at us. These are the bones of beasts and monsters, stripped by carrion eaters but it is as if the flesh they

220

once wore is of no consequence. They are more terrible without it.

Zamora carefully steps around a curved horn that juts from a skull as large as her upper body. A second horn has been shattered halfway up its stem.

"Hunting giants is no task for boys or women," Otu says and though I know he insults me and the other women, he does not do it to be a jerk; it is his way of saying that the task he pretends we'll soon undertake is difficult. To think that he's slain beasts such as these, with spear and arrow, to think that over the generations these bones have accumulated, dragged here by men doing what should have been impossible.

I admit it, there's a flare of pride at the thought that my husband is capable of killing such creatures. It is a primitive pride, one that I'd not have thought still existed in my very modern genetic code. I wonder if Salva would be capable of such a feat. I flush, feeling guilty for thinking such a thing.

Yet there is a difference. Otu did not kill a giant on his own, no task on Terrasta is ever succeeded at without help from others. On Earth it is different. Salva's father and grandfather (not their workforce, their advisers, their investors) will always be credited with Gehum's successes, as shall any future success be attributed to Salva himself. Not even Kono takes full credit for the kills he makes.

They are the clan's kills.

The altar of dark logs is carried by four massive leg bones, pounded into the earth and angled away from one another, pointing up. Otu sets the offering on the altar and despite the weight of the meat, the bones do not move at all and I wonder how deep the legs must penetrate the earth.

Suddenly the night's darkness is disrupted by brilliant flashes of light. I gawk at the unexpected light show but my shock is nothing compared with Otu and Zamora's piety. They fall to their knees and bow their heads.

I'm as surprised as they but less inclined to blind obedience (not my society's way, unless the obedience is the voluntary kind, like from effective advertisement) and so I stare at the hill instead. I'm rewarded with a glimpse of a shadow disappearing into the woods and I grin. Still, I lower myself to the ground, with the others. No reason to be disrespectful.

"The magician was right," Otu whispers when he rises a few moments later. "The godlings approve."

Zamora's grins now and I don't have the heart to tell them that I saw their magician on the ridge. That the birdwoman (and not the godlings) is responsible for the light show and that the meat will disappear tonight because she has taken it home to eat.

They are a simple people. But their simplicity serves my purpose now.

I might not be surprised by the birdwoman's *magic* but I am shocked when Zamora reaches for my hand on the walk back to the village.

"I've never seen godlings before," she says.

Her hand holding changes everything. Maybe these people are simple. Maybe their dependence makes them unsophisticated, but her friendship, her inclusion of me, this shared moment, it makes me long for more.

Patience is not my virtue. It is not sufficient for me to wait for my inevitable rescue and my return to proper society. I am alone but for this fleeting moment I am not. I've been included, in this.

Time to reciprocate.

CHAPTER 20

A Gal and Her Robot

"What do you want to show me?"

"Not far now, Zamora." I speak loud to be heard over the crackling of my torch. We are at the edge of the Fen, with a cloud covered night sky above us. I've hardly slept, waking before sunrise, anxious and uncertain of my decision, but the need I have to strengthen this growing bond between us is irresistible. And I might not have another chance, at least for a while, because I think I'll need to head again to the menses lodge, soon.

I need to give her my secret, so that she understands how important her friendship is to me. How important that we women have something the men do not. There's something gentler and more satisfying living in a world where women are free to be close to one another and I've missed it.

"Do you know much about the birdwoman, your magician?" I ask, to fill the silence.

"Otu tells me she had a husband, who died many, many years ago. A son too, he died as well, and when he did, she apprenticed to the clan's magician, succeeding him, when he passed."

I shudder at the thought of the poor woman's loss, and, in an attempt to find reason behind the birdwoman's strangeness, I ask Zamora if her son died young.

She shakes her head. "He was a man, Promoted, even, which is rare, for this clan. Not long after he returned he was lost, during a hunt in a snowstorm, to the north. They never found him."

"When was this?"

Zamora shrugs. "Long before my time here. But the magician, she's much the same as any other. My clan has one, his name is Veers. He doesn't listen to the birds, but he burns bones and sees godling whispers in their smoke. He decides when to travel to the coast for winter and when to return, when marriages are most auspicious and what names the godlings desire for the children."

We might have talked more but we've reached Doser and our conversation trails away at the sight of him. Her expression is the same as when we witnessed the birdwoman's fireworks.

Zamora asks, "A godling? Here?"

Doser hovers in front of us, looking first at

Zamora, then at me, his eye glowing brilliantly, the moonlight dim and washed out by the cloud cover. The damage the giant did to him has not healed completely but it does not dampen his effect on Zamora.

What he says, does. "I'm not a godling."

Zamora stumbles backwards.

"Doser is my secret," I say, "But he is not a godling. He is a thing, made. By people. Like a spear or a bow."

"He is not at all like a spear or a bow, Miranda."

Doser snort-chirps. "Now that she has seen me, she must die, you know that, Miranda."

Zamora glances at me, her eyes wider, her lips trembling.

"Never mind him. He's a grouch. We are not killing anybody." There's nothing Doser can do. Once seen he cannot be unseen. We spend almost an hour with the robot, him dutifully answering Zamora's questions though remaining vague enough that he tells her nothing important. Afterwards, we walk back to the lodge, hand in hand, Zamora begging to see him again. I promise to oblige her. After all, this is what friends do.

"You are one of them," she says as we near the village.

"A what?"

"A magician."

"No," I protest, "I am just a woman."

That night I sleep soundly, not missing the sweet oblivion of the drugs I no longer take. In

226

my dreaming I see Zamora's face, her delight, her almost rapture. I know that tomorrow my world will be all the better for the sharing of this secret.

I wake smiling and excited to embrace the day. I've slept late but I still expect to find Otu asleep, still expect to help Zamora with breakfast. I'm eager to talk about our shared secret.

What I do not expect is to have Otu standing over my bed, glaring down at me. Zamora is at his side. I'm only half awake, not entirely returned from the pleasantness of my dreams when he kicks me in the ribs.

"Where is it?" he demands.

"What?" I mumble. Otu grasps me by the shoulder and lifts me. I stumble, catching a post for balance. Zamora stares at me.

"Just tell him." I flush with understanding: she's revealed our secret.

"You have lied to me, wife." Otu raises his hand. I think of the revolver in the marriage box, think that now, I might actually need it to protect myself. But I can hardly reach it in time and even if I do what would I do with it. Kill him? Kill Zamora? Kill everybody?

"Please, stop, I'll tell."

Otu waits, arm poised. Just as I open my mouth I waver, swaying as a wave of nausea overwhelms me. And then I puke.

"A wife, even if just a second wife, hides no secrets from her husband," Zamora whispers to me. We lag behind Otu again. Clouds dampen the sun but the way is bright enough. Still, my world is grayer somehow, despite the light.

"Go to hell." She won't understand the last word, but she gets the point, I'm sure. My stomach churns, weakening my bravado. It is as if my insides are as conflicted as my mind — I've vomited three times since Zamora betrayed me. (At least few funeral pyres burn, I doubt I'd be doing anything but vomiting if I have to smell more of that.)

The wind tugs at my clothing as we reach the Fen. Here, Otu wavers, worrying about drawing too close to the menses lodge, but when I lead him past that, into the Fen itself, he relaxes some. Most of the trees near us are conifers and their needles last all winter, but here and there a few leaf-bearing trees sport yellowing leaves. The shortened spring and summer make it imperative that we set off on the trek to the Tower, soon. How miserable will the coming fall be on this planet?

Otu's ambition worries me. The sickness has run its course yet that does not dampen his inclination, his desire to explore the Tower. This has grown well past curing the plague. I hope that Doser satisfies my husband's curiosity without introducing any delays. I also hope that we do not stumble across the giant that attacked my robot. The giant I have never warned anyone about.

"Wait here," Otu says, gesturing to Zamora but not me. I don't look at her. She's so sure that she's done the right thing and I'm more than pleased that Otu excludes her from this. He guides me by the shoulder.

Of course he's not leaving Zamora behind as punishment. She's watching for intruders. And he's not gentle with me at all; he shoves me forward until we near the location and I call out for Doser. The robot responds and rises before us. If he had eyes, proper eyes, like a human, I'm sure he would have rolled them upon seeing Otu standing there.

"Yet another," Doser mutters, completely oblivious to the fear flickering across Otu's face. The man's large hand has wrapped around the knife at his belt and I'm sure he's regretting not bringing his spear.

"She spoke the truth," he says, his voice weak, but I'm not sure he's referring to me or the bitch, Zamora. Otu paces a careful circle around the robot, stepping gingerly, finding safe footing in the marsh without looking down. "Like a child's puppet."

"No," I say before Doser is rude, "I do not control him."

"Impossible," Otu says and there in the filtered marsh light I see astonishment on the face of this hardened hunter. Doser is beyond the man's understanding.

"Now, please, may I kill them?"

Otu pulls his knife free.

"No, Doser, that isn't necessary."

"Twice now you've compromised us, Miranda," Doser says, ignoring Otu and his weapon, "I might as well swoop down into the village itself and reveal myself. Maybe these savages might even worship me, as one of their silly godlings. Wouldn't that be sweet?"

Otu snarls, "Do not consider it, *golem*."

"Relax," I say, though I'm not feeling well enough to really intervene if the two of them start a proper fight. "Otu wants confirmation that what I've told him is true."

"Can he do it?" Otu asks.

"Do what?" I'm really feeling dizzy and so I reach for a nearby tree, for support, ignoring the sticky sap my palm slides across. I am on shaky ground, not just figuratively, caught between the savage and the robot and the baggage of the worlds both carry.

"Can he kill me?" I stare at the man, seeing hunger and not fear in his eyes. He's not worried about himself, he's wondering if Doser, if the robot, is a sufficient weapon, the leverage he needs to oust Kono.

"Such animals," Doser says, "such beastly things. Obsessed with war."

"Not war." I defend my husband, though I'm not sure why I bother. "It is about survival."

Otu nods. "She understands that I'm a better leader than Kono. The man is too impulsive and dangerous."

My husband lowers his knife. Perhaps he does not think Doser is capable of following through with his threat. Which is close to the

230

truth. The robot has no weapons, though I imagine he might make a nuisance of himself, if he tries.

The rain is falling now and I think the chill water spraying across my face is the only thing keeping me on my feet. I'm at a loss. I don't know what to do and I long for the oblivion of my former life. All I want to do is go home, not my mat on the floor of Otu's lodge, but home, my real home.

"Doser will help us reach the Tower," I say.

"But if there's no need—"

"There's a need," I snap back, interrupting my husband; my skull has clamped too tight around my brain. Otu's eyes widen. Then he lunges at me.

Doser misunderstands, as do I. The robot swats at Otu and his retractable claw is not as fragile as it looks. Otu is knocked sideways. I press my back against the sticky tree, unable to stop either robot or man as Otu slashes at Doser with his knife.

The robot dips away and Otu screams that I'm about to fall and I'm wondering whether he's actually trying to protect me when dizziness overwhelms me and I pitch forward, into the Fen.

Otu may not have caught me but he does retrieve me from the Fen and carry me towards the village. The rain wakens me before we reach it.

"It's this stormcurse, it makes us all weak," Otu assures me, carrying me like a child as we meet up with Zamora and leave Doser at the edge of the Fen. Zamora promises to come back and tell the robot how I fare.

Otu carries me the rest of the way, into our lodge. Then he sets me down and I fall into a proper sleep. When I wake, it is dark outside, only the hearthfire casting light. Zamora and Otu sit beside me, spooning soup from wooden bowls, their heads bowed together, murmuring as they watch over me.

I turn my head to the other side and startle.

The birdwoman stares at me. I realize that I've been undressed and redressed, in warm clothes, and that I'm beneath what seems to be all the blankets we own. The old woman smiles and her birds watch me with interest, it makes her seem to be a creature with many, many, eyes.

"She's awake," the magician says and I wish she didn't because Otu fusses, asking me question after question and I don't know the answers. I don't understand what's wrong with me, why I still feel gross and light headed. I don't know and I can't assure him I am well. The only good that comes from his attention is that I know it frustrates Zamora. When she rests her palm on my forehead, I slap her hand away. The birdwoman seems surprised at this but does not comment as Otu's first wife retreats to the other side of the lodge and busies herself with menial task.

232

"What's wrong with Miranda?" Otu asks.

The birdwoman shrugs. "I think I know, but I must finish my examinations alone."

Otu's eyes narrow, as if he suspects some trick from her, as if he's worried about leaving me alone with a stranger, as if I'm in the habit of blurting out my secrets to one and all, but finally he gives his consent and he and Zamora step out.

The birdwoman examines me in ways I'd rather not be examined; lifting my skirts and poking and prodding. I don't have much to do as I lie there except watch her. Staring at her chest I realize there are fewer birds perched on her than usual. The orange bird, my bird, is missing too and a few of those that remain appear lethargic.

"Where are the others?" I reach to stroke a tiny brown bird head.

"Sick or vanished." There's such sadness in her voice, that my eyes fill with tears. "Some of them, like yours, have flown away, many others have died. Nidawi has turned the godlings against us."

What follows is silence broken only by the birdwoman's occasional cluck of tongue against teeth. When she really starts getting into her examinations, pushing here and prodding there, I need to keep on talking, so I'm not thinking about what she is doing or why she is doing it.

(And for the record, she hasn't got the warmest of fingers.)

"I forgot to thank you, for the marriage

box."

She looks up at me and really, I'd rather she didn't, given what she's doing. "You could not be married, without one."

"But the gifts, they were… kind."

"Are they not yours?" She looks down again. "I did not know what else to give a woman who has fallen from the sky, except that which fell with her."

I have no reply for that, clearly she does not understand the significance. Mother's journal is mostly useless to me but the revolver, if I'm bold enough to use it, might change everything. Maybe it replaces the leverage I've lost, now that Otu and Zamora know about Doser.

Eventually the birdwoman finishes, wiping her hands on her dress as I make myself proper again.

"Miranda from the Sky, you are a mystery, to me. First you arrive and our elders sicken, die, but the birds sing in your favor, saving you. But then the birds themselves wither, the godlings silenced. Only now, on this day, am I relieved that I was right earlier. Only now do I see the hope I nurtured before, fulfilled."

"I don't understand." For a while I've thought of the birdwoman as an ally but if she blames me for her dying birds and for the sickness, then I am uncertain.

"I've been watching you; your blood war, it is late, is it not?"

I blush. Why yes, now that you mention it, it appears to be so, thank you for paying attention to such an awkward (and private) thing.

"Yeah." I almost add a "so what" but I'm not an idiot, because I figure out what she means and my eyes widen.

"Yours will be the first child born to the clan in years."

CHAPTER 21

A Child of the Clan

Now Salva will know. He'll know everything that has happened to me. No drugs, no forgetting, can hide a child. Something is growing inside me and I don't want it, I don't want it all.

I'm alone; the birdwoman is outside collecting Otu and Zamora and I can't even ask her to end the pregnancy, she'd never consider it, not given the sterility that afflicts the clan. She might even insist on having me watched, supervised. A new baby is too important to the clan. The time has passed when I might have prevented this (not that I know how without the use of drugs).

If I'm to live, so must it.

The birdwoman leads them in and I hear her tell Otu and Zamora as they step across the threshold. My husband's face changes in a way I never would have expected. The hard lines fade, his eyes brighten, and he even smiles, a real smile, not the kind men use when joking around the common's fire, where humor is as much a part of the daily tugging and shoving that is integral to their hierarchical society. It is Zamora's reaction that gives me the most pleasure. Her lips tremble and her eyes fall to her hands, which twist and pull at each another. She is the first to offer congratulations, though tersely, and then she steps away, turns her back, and starts preparing our meal.

Otu helps me to my feet, my hands clasped in his.

"I waited long to marry," he says, "taking Zamora into my bed long after our women proved themselves barren. I thought she and I might be blessed, but now it does not matter. You will give me a son!"

I don't know what to say but I really don't like how he's staring at my belly. He's too eager.

"Fortune falls again in our favor," the birdwoman says. "Many blessings to your hearth."

She turns, as if to leave, but Otu stops her, releasing me, to focus his attention on her.

"Magician, I wish to beg your indulgence in keeping this matter private, for now."

I've never seen the birdwoman surprised but even the birds sense her discomfort, stopping their pruning and murmuring, as they glare at Otu.

"A new child must be celebrated and—"

He wags his finger. "I must be the first to announce it. I... I need to prepare a feast, in honor of him."

Him? Doesn't he know that Terrastan women only bear girls? (Or almost, always, anyways.) And why doesn't he want to tell anybody?

"I save this news, for you to share, Otu Wickettson."

The hide parts abruptly, startling all of us, as Kono strides in, a strange look on his face that makes me wonder if he has been eavesdropping for some time.

"What news is this?"

Otu bristles. "It is a private matter, Kono, between my hearth and the godlings."

Kono muscles his way in, four of his advisers trailing him, the impulsive young men who have replaced wiser voices.

"Such a private matter that *our clan's* magician, is here?"

Otu fidgets, his biceps extending as he presses his hands together, as if to still his desire to wrap his hands around Kono's neck and squeeze. Though Kono is the taller of the two my husband is thicker and wider and I do not think the contest would be decided before it began.

But with Kono's allies here it would be a one sided match.

"I saw you, carrying your slave," Kono says, his voice quiet. "As *headman*, I am concerned."

I'm not a slave anymore, of course, but I

know well enough not to correct Kono. And I know his concern is just yacking. I glance at my marriage box, set beside Zamora's. Though hers is full of practical items, mine has a revolver. Which might even the odds. I seriously consider it in the half second before Otu, shoulders slumped, speaks.

"My wife, is with child."

Every man, except Kono, stares past me, to Zamora. Otu corrects their gaze by pointing at me. What flickers across Kono's face I won't ever know for certain but his complexion darkens. He recovers quickly.

"A child! Our clan shall have a new child!" He clasps Otu by the forearm, drawing my husband in for a hug and then the other men do the same. Otu accepts their blessings but I suspect it's all a charade.

"Because of this… blessing," Otu says, "I wish to set off on the hunt, as soon as possible."

"The hunt?" Kono says, and the concern in his voice is definitely false. "Think of your wife, your child. You are to be a father. Considering the stormcurse's wrath this summer I think the hunt too dangerous."

"But the giant—"

"Is far from us. Save your spears for the spring," he says, "and enjoy the spoils the godlings have brought into your lodge."

Kono turns away as more men and women enter the lodge, offering congratulations and ruining all our plans. The spontaneous well wishing does not end for hours, but when it does, when we are alone again, Otu is in a dark mood.

"Maybe it is for the best," Zamora says and in an eye blink Otu strides across the room and slaps her across the face, sending her sprawling to the floor. I'm so startled that I almost drop the cooling mug of broth I've been holding (all night the women have been handing me things to eat and drink as if the creature inside me is a ravenous beast).

I almost say something, to her, to him, but I think better of it and keep to myself. I sit beside where I've set grandmother's urn on the floor, just taking comfort in the dead woman's presence.

You will have a great grandchild.

I am more alone than ever, despite our lodge hosting visitor after visitor over the following days. As the bruise on Zamora's face darkens and then lightens, I feel as if I am the only woman in all the world. If the clan knew I did not want this child I suspect they'd fall over, dead from shock. Had I ever considered a child, I would have conceived it using Salva's genetic material. Who knows what awfulness lurks inside Otu's genes? Unnatural height or near sightedness or freckles.

I shudder. If I were a wiser woman I might have learned to prevent the pregnancy in the first place but I've lived all my life taking pills and injections. Yes, obviously, I knew that coupling leads to pregnancy but it should have been a rarer event, right? Otu has only bedded me a few times.

A small lodge is a lonely place to be when you hate the woman you share it with. Better if Otu and I were gone from here, if Kono had not forbidden us. Then Zamora would be here and I'd be halfway to home.

A handful of days then a week and then another passes and the leafs yellow and Zamora's bruise fades completely, though I know I'll never forget Otu's violence. Nor will she. We are constantly reminded of his agitation. His plans for claiming the clan have been thwarted and the potential for another explosion is always there. When Otu does speak it is to make demands or extract information from me and he often takes me to the Fen, to interrogate Doser.

(Yet his problems are nothing compared with mine. To think I must birth a child with only these savages to help me, without the bliss of medicated delivery. I will not sleep soundly until it is done, I know I won't.)

One evening after successfully avoiding Zamora for weeks (a difficult feat given the cramped lodge we share), she sits down beside me.

Mother's tablet has proven itself somewhat useful, for in those rare moments when neither Zamora or I are engaged in chores (you wouldn't believe how much work our robots back home take on for us!) I use the tablet as a shield. I sit with it in my lap and unsnap the earbuds from their divot on the tablet's underside and I listen to music.

Mother has (had) shitty taste.

I don't think there's harm in thinking that about her, now. It is not disrespectful, but mere fact. Still, the music she listened to (something called jazz) reminds me of her and my world. It also does a brilliant job of muffling outside noise, like the question Zamora asks now.

After she refuses to leave me alone, I remove a bud and ask her to repeat herself.

"What is that?" she asks.

"Nothing."

"Oh," she says but does not move away, just sits there, sliding a stray lock of her blond hair away from her eyes. I might move outside, find a quiet place to be alone, but chances are that a man might notice and find work for me or the women might gather and fawn over the *thing* growing inside me.

Better Zamora's attention than all the others.

"It is music," I say and then after failing to explain it to her I place the earbud against her ear, even knowing I can't wash it before I return it to my own. This place is changing me and not for the better.

Her eyes widen and she recoils, only to draw herself close again. "Where's the singer?"

"Inside." I tap the tablet. This doesn't seem to make the experience any less amazing for her and she's soon asking me question after question and seeing no harm in giving her answers, I do.

"The birdwoman returned this to me, in my marriage box," I say. "It belonged to my mother."

And I don't know why exactly I do it but I show her the toggles on the side and how to flip through tracks and adjust the volume. She's delighted and this pleases me.

"I have something to show you too." She hands the bud back to me and crosses the floor to open her marriage chest. When she returns she sets a folded bundle, tied with sinew, in front of me. She tugs on the string and opens it. Inside are clothes: tiny trousers, tiny dresses, tiny tunics, even tiny moccasins.

"I started making these, soon after my marriage."

She doesn't have to say more. She is Otu's wife and she wanted to bring his children into the world and she failed, though I'll hardly bond with her by explaining how much I wish I *was not* pregnant.

"These are for you."

"Thank you, but you might—"

She shakes her head. "I won't. Maybe making these clothes, being sure I'd soon be a mother, maybe it discouraged the godlings. Maybe I was too vain, too proud."

Zamora wronged me, really wronged me, and I still can't help thinking that if she had not told Otu about Doser my pregnancy would not have been discovered this early. Kono would not have forbidden us from leaving the village. But I am the weakest of all my family and I put my arm around her shoulders and thank her for the tiny clothes.

We spend the rest of the day listening to music and pawing through the clothes, me commenting on her stitch work (something I still suck at) and the beading on the little dresses. There is clothing for either a boy or a girl; Zamora was prepared.

It is well past dark when Otu returns, startling us. Zamora springs to her feet, to see if our husband has need of us, and he does. He barks orders and soon we are both rushing here and there, filling his traveling sack with clothing and food and water. He doesn't say anything to us, other than telling us he needs provisions for several days. Mostly he just mutters, staring at our western wall, glaring at the headman's lodge.

Then he sits by the door, waiting, until the general evening chatter of the clan fades, outside. Eventually I fall asleep, my back against a wall, near the hearthfire, for fall's cool winds have begun to scour our village.

When I wake Otu is gone. Zamora is still sleeping, on the other side of the hearthfire which now has only coals. For almost an hour I am alone with my thoughts and mother's tablet. I keep the screen dimmed, trying to cajole another month or two of battery life from it;

this sacrifice does not bother me at all, I have no interest in reading mother's journals. I spend my morning listening to music and trying to avoid wondering where Otu has went.

Zamora rises, staring long and hard at the empty spot where Otu should have slept. I pull the ear buds out of my ears.

"He's gone," I say.

"Kono shames our husband."

"By refusing to let him hunt the giant?"

"Kono should not have told Otu how to care for his women, not in front of the other men," she says. She touches her cheek, where he struck her, but I doubt she realizes she does it.

"Where is he?"

"Hunting?" By the way she shrugs I'm not sure she believes that. I don't. It is too dangerous for hunters to hunt on their own. And a new worry appears: what if Otu stumbles across the giant that attacked Doser? He will not expect a monster to be so close to our village, especially if he's blinded by rage.

I don't tell Zamora any of this.

I leave and collect water for the stew we'll eat and spend some time near the river, admiring the squirrels foraging and dodging the yellow leaves falling around them like soldiers crossing a battlefield. The little creatures amuse me, their antics more random than the plaything robots I owned during childhood. The artificial intelligence driving the robots simply wouldn't allow itself to be as bizarre as these furry tailed critters. My smile fades when I see Kono's first wife approach, carrying empty buckets.

"Otu is not at the men's fire," she says, in lieu of greeting.

"He's not?"

She shakes her head. "Kono wants to speak to him. Where is he?"

"It is not a wife's place to question her husband's whereabouts." I leave her and the squirrels and rush back to my lodge to avoid more questions.

Another day passes and I sneak off to the Fen, to ask Doser if he has seen Otu.

"You must search for him," I tell my robot. I am vulnerable without Otu.

"Whatever," Doser says, but I know he'll obey. I hasten home, in case Otu has returned.

On the third day of Otu's absence, Kono himself comes to our lodge and we finally admit that we do not know where Otu is. Kono berates us and demands an explanation but we don't know, we only have our guesses and I refuse to say what I think: that Otu has left for the Tower, without me, that he thinks he might find his way inside it, that he thinks he will find weapons to wrestle the clan's leadership from Kono.

"If your man has disobeyed me," Kono says, "he will be punished."

"Punished?"

Now Kono smiles and I think maybe he knew exactly what he was doing when he shamed Otu. "Exile."

Zamora clutches the centerpost and leans against it. I move to stand beside her, not quite understanding what she already has.

"And us?" she asks.

"Another man, a more capable man, will take on the responsibility of tending to Otu's wives," Kono says, "and the clan's newest child."

He leaves us with that threat but he is not the last visitor of the evening.

CHAPTER 22

Bringing Our Husband Home

A tapping across my forehead wakes me from a restless slumber. I open my eyes, slowly.

"Zamora, what—" I stop, because it is Doser that hovers over me; Zamora yet sleeps. The robot's lights are dim and he's barely visible in the afterglow of the depleted hearthfire.

"I found your husband, out past the Fen"

Before I can respond, Zamora wakes; she has slept poorly (and lightly) since Otu's disappearance. "Our husband?" She rises, groggily, and settles beside me.

"Is he well?" I ask.

"He found the giant."

Zamora understands, before I, what this means, and when she asks if he is dead, Doser bobs in confirmation. Suddenly, irrevocably, my world has turned upside down again. With Otu dead I am not a wife, I am not protected. Zamora has a more pronounced reaction, releasing a rattling moan. I place my hand on her shoulder and urge her to silence. Tears stream down her face; she truly mourns him.

(I do not. Otu might be a better man than the other savages, but his running off and getting killed proves his selfishness. He promised to protect me and now he has abandoned me.)

"We must return his body," Zamora says, "where did he fall?"

Doser's dome pops open and reveals a viewscreen about the size of a commoner's phone. A still image shows two rivers meeting headlong, leaving a triangle of rocky beach between them. The merged rivers flow on, tumbling down a waterfall, into a gorge below, surrounded by thick forests and orange-brown walls of stone. This entire view seems as if it has been shoved into the narrowing part of a funnel, the rivers, the forest, the rocks, all jumbled together.

"We must not let Kono know," I say, as I search the screen for Otu's body. Zamora finds him first, touching the screen with her index finger and then I notice his legs sticking out from behind a jumbled pile of river scoured logs.

"That's to the south, where the rivers join," Zamora says. "There's sturgeon there, in the

spring, come up from the bay. We fish there."
She rattles off these points, all the while
touching the screen, as if somehow, through a
transference birthed by technology and magic,
she might comfort her dead husband's soul.

"Turn it off."

The screen slides away.

"We must go, now."

"We cannot, Zamora." I hold her by the
hand. "If Kono knows… you heard what he
said. He'll claim us, I know he will."

Her eyes narrow. "You are fearful, Miranda,
when instead, you must grieve. A proper wife
mourns her husband, thinks of him above
herself."

Why does she not understand how stupid
her comment is? The women have convinced
themselves they are inferior to men and they
always put men's needs above their own,
devaluing themselves. It is utterly ridiculous.

"We need a few days—"

"A few days and Nidawi, the giant woman,
she'll take his soulspirit! A few days and Otu
will be devoured by that mad bitch and we'll be
cursed by him, as we'll deserve. I will not have
that haunt me, Miranda."

Her beliefs control her and I feel pity for her
and her pathetic society.

She's heading towards the door and I grab
her by the arm, spinning her back, staring at
her. She does not understand how serious this
is. That this might be my final chance, to
escape.

"Give me a few minutes, Zamora."

Instead she screams, an echo of the mourning cries I've been listening to since I arrived at this horrid village. Doser, who has been watching our altercation, turns to me.

"What now?" he asks.

"I don't know." I glare at Zamora. She is defiant and surely believes that she is doing the right thing. Yet she is wrong. "For now, hide again, Doser."

The robot flees as the village erupts with life.

By morning the men are prepared to recover Otu's body. The only concession Zamora has given me is that she has lied about how she learned of his death, telling the clan a story about how she dreamed of our husband's death. In my world she would have been mocked but the savages take dreams seriously. Zamora and I are to accompany the men, as is the way of the clan, for it is our responsibility to prepare his body for the pyre.

I'm the last to clamber from the woods and onto the river shore, the last to see Otu's broken spear and his carrying sack torn in two. The last to cross the thick tree the clan felled many years in the past to serve as a bridge across the first river, leading to the narrow strip of land between both bodies of water. The last to step foot on this paltry island and see my dead husband.

Kono gestures to us women to deal with the

body as he and his men search the area, scouting for the giant. Months ago I had never seen a dead body but I'm mostly numb as I stare down at this man, a man I've been intimate with, a man that I believed was my salvation. He's been torn apart at the waist, disemboweled, and partly eaten. Mercifully, Zamora performs most of the preparations herself.

Morning bleeds into afternoon and I'm pleased when the rain falls because it makes it easier to clean Otu's gore from our hands and arms.

"After we honor our brother's soulspirit, we shall hunt this giant! We shall kill this giant!" Kono declares and the men cheer. They scout the area, looking at the scuff marks on the nearby logs and the deep impressions made by the giant's feet in the river rock as we wrap our husband in a hide Zamora carried here.

I'm having a hard time focusing on this last part of our task because I'm studying this strange juxtaposition of forest, rock and river. And I'm wondering.

"How close, are we?"

Zamora stares at me, blankly. "Close?"

"To the sea."

She must believe me callous, what with our husband rolled up before us, but I'm thinking that maybe with everybody distracted, this might be my chance. There must be another way out of the valley: these conjoined rivers have to exit somewhere.

"Unless your people walk on water," she says, "it is impossible. The river carves through the granite ahead, but there's no shore, just rock and water. No path for man, or woman."

I shrug, disappointed but she's not finished. "And," she says, her voice rising higher, "we have a husband to mourn."

I nod instead of speaking but I'm not done with this idea. The giant found its way into the clan's valley and it could not have done this by taking the pass that the scouts guard. Which means it used the river.

We return home but do not enter the village, instead heading towards the pyre. The birdwoman is already waiting for us there and so is the entire village. She nods in greeting but I startle. Not because I did not expect her here (obviously, she must oversee the funeral ceremony) but because of her birds.

They are all gone.

"It is a poor omen," the magician says to me, after Otu's soulspirit has been set free. We are on the way back to the village but lag behind the other villagers, lingering at the crossroads, the large beaten path leading to the village splitting off, a lighter traveled trail that I decide must lead to the birdwoman's residence. Not a particularly difficult realization for me to make given that she has stepped off of my trail, to stand upon this other.

I am only half paying attention to her

because the stench of Otu's burnt corpse lingers in the air, the wind being particularly unkind, blowing it village-ward. If I were superstitious I might even entertain the notion that the black smoke, his soulspirit, is following me, as if accusing me of inadequate grief. Or accusing me of causing his death.

I knew about the giant in the Fen and didn't tell. In fact I *had* hoped somebody would die. But a somebody like Kono; not Otu.

"The last three of my birds died last night. As if they all agreed to pass on together."

I can only shake my head and offer her sympathy.

She says, "All things happen because the godlings want them to. Perhaps the birds die to remind me that it will soon be my time."

"I'm sure that's not true," I say. Though I'm more worried over my own fate I am sorry for her. She's lost a husband and a son and she's lived most of her life isolated. She's scared and she can't admit that to anybody, except me. She's an outsider as much as I am.

"I have been foolish," she says and if there's anybody in the clan who shouldn't be called such, it is she. She ignores my protest, pushing on. "You must come and visit me tomorrow. You have no husband now." When I don't make the connection, between visiting her and my not having a husband she smiles, shakes her head. "Miranda From the Sky, every clan needs a magician." I'm stunned and shocked and maybe even flabbergasted.

"Me?"

It is a generous offer. Knowing even a portion of what the magician knows would secure me a future with the clan, a future that does not involve becoming Kono's wife.

"Promise me, tomorrow, after first light, that you'll come here."

I give her this promise but I know I'll break it. I must leave, as I should have left long ago. The birdwoman has shown me kindness, but I do not belong here. There's too much that is outside of my control, if I remain.

And now I know that there's another way out of this valley.

CHAPTER 23

A New Journey
Begins

I'm coming home, Mr. Durand. That's a promise. Don't you worry about me, I have it all figured out. I'm excited and happy for the first time in a long time. There... there is stuff I can't tell you now, but that doesn't matter, does it? We'll be reunited and together, somehow, we'll figure out the rest.

You'll forgive me if I do not explain it all, won't you? A lady must have her secrets. And despite this brutal planet, I am still a lady, with hope, still your lady?

It has been a long journey but it is near an end and more than anything else I must be reunited with you. Then, and only then, will my world be put right.

After speaking with the magician I hurried to the Fen and told Doser my plan and now I've hurried back to the village. Those were not more mere words I spoke to Salva. They are truths, signs that my conviction is indomitable now.

Packing without Zamora realizing what I'm doing is made all the easier when the men return, late in the evening. They have been hunting the giant since the moment the birdwoman said her last words over Otu's pyre and now, barely a handful of hours later, the excited cries outside my lodge tell me they have succeeded.

Zamora tells me that the women will stand over the giant while the men cleanse themselves from the hunt. Afterwards there will be another ceremony to honor Otu. I know she's telling me these things so that I will join her outside but when she rushes from the lodge I scurry about, taking advantage of her absence.

I stuff a leather satchel with dried meat and graincakes and I take two empty flasks that I'll fill at the river. I steal a stone blade that Zamora won't miss. And a birchbark pot. And a handful of other utensils and things, not so much that I'll be weighed down. I take a spare dress and an old leather wrap, once a cloak but worn now and used mostly as a floor covering. Zamora won't notice it, as long as I keep the fire low, the light dim. I'll be gone before she wakes, before my scheduled appointment with the magician.

257

I take three other things with me. Three things that don't belong on Terrasta. The revolver, the journal, and grandmother's ashes. I set the bulging satchel beside my bedroll.

A half hour has passed but the cheering of the women hasn't diminished and curiosity encourages me to join the others. It will also help alleviate any suspicion, I think, if I am with them and not hiding in here on my own. The clan does not trust hiders and avoiders.

The staked and lit torches cast long shadows over the commons and the slain giant. I'm not sure what I expected. From hearing the monster on the beach to Doser's stone throwing to the attack against the robot, I've been building a picture in my mind of what giants must look like.

I've been wrong.

The creature is almost twice as tall as Kono and a horn grows from its head, though not a horn like a unicorn, this shaft of bone is bent and twisted back on its self several times, terminating into several sharp tips. Thin brown-black fur covers his body, but not so much that I can't tell that it was male.

"It's almost a man," I say. Zamora, who stands at the giant's head, gives me an odd look. I add, somewhat sheepishly, "I thought it would be more like an animal."

"It is an animal."

The crowd is no longer cheering, most have withdrawn to the edge of the torch cast light, but in the moment of silence that lingers between Zamora and myself, a mother cajoles his son to step forward and the boy does, stabbing the giant's thigh with a half spear. The crowd murmurs approval and the boy falls back into place, in the crowd.

Zamora gives him a smile, but turns her attention back to me. "No giant is the same as any other, but they are always shaped in man's image. Nidawi's curse twists flesh and blackens souls."

No curse enacted this transformation, I think. Outrageous genetic mutations have shaped this giant. Throughout centuries of space travel humankind has found no evidence for sentient life on other planets, but it seems that Gehum has created their own.

The giant's cheek bones are gracile, curving away from a slightly elongated nose. From the side the profile is reminiscent of the woodland deer the hunters stalk. I point that out to Zamora and she nods.

"When an animal is slain but the proper rites not observed, the creature returns, a blend of what it was and of the man who slew it without honoring it."

I listen to the stories the women tell, while the men prepare for the next part of the ceremony. They speak of past hunts and of Otu's exploits. They explain to the precious few children why it is important to honor the dead, both human and animal, using the slain beast to illustrate their points. Throughout it all they blame Kal's clan, despite Zamora standing right there.

I grow tense as the men return and form a circle around the women but to my surprise they just stand and listen, rare for a man to do, when in the presence of a woman who is speaking; generally they interrupt, berate. Still, the gaze of almost every man there, lingers over me.

I'm pregnant, I can do what no other woman in the clan can. If the child is healthy I'll be the most important woman in the clan. Either through training to be a magician or proving my worth with my uterus, I might actually attain significant prestige and power over these savages.

I haven't really considered it before but it changes nothing. After Zamora and I return to our empty lodge I turn my music on and sit there, watching her slide under her sleeping skins without undressing, watching her fall into a deep, deserved sleep.

I wait several hours and when I'm sure there's nobody awake outside I remove my headphones and stuff them and mother's journal into the satchel. I dress and keep watch on Zamora. Her hair has fallen partly over her face but it is impossible not to see the tear streaks on her cheeks. In a different situation I might have spent the night comforting her but I am now committed to my exodus.

I sling the satchel's strap over my shoulder, finding the weight tolerable and I'm about to step outside when Zamora's eyes pop open. I realize instantly I haven't woken her, that she's been lying awake. Waiting.

"Where are you going?" she asks.

All it will take is a scream and she'll ruin it all, again.

"For a walk."

Zamora shakes her head. "You lie, Miranda."

I am flustered but she's smiling and I don't understand why. She rises from bed and now I'm wondering if her falling asleep with her clothes on was as accidental as it seemed. Had she known my intentions?

I don't answer. I can't, not really. Instead, I bite my lip and wait.

"While Otu lived I never would have dared."

"Dare what?"

"To return to my clan."

"But earlier—"

"I had to honor my dead husband. But that is done. And now another man will take me as wife. A man who might have been one of those who killed Kal. How can I share my bed with such?"

I am beyond ecstatic. Zamora knows how to survive on Terrasta.

"I must go to the Tower," I say. I expect her to argue with me and I see she wants to because her eyes widen and her mouth opens, but she doesn't. She stops herself.

"We will share a trail, for much of the way,"

261

she says. "It is better than going alone." We'll split up, later, is what she means.

It takes Zamora ten minutes to prepare her own satchel and then we sneak out of the village.

"About time," Doser declares when we reach the Fen and reveal our plan to him. Zamora shakes her head when I explain the route I intend to take and not just because she's hesitant to return to where Otu was slain.

"I told you before, Miranda. Unless you are fish or bird, there is no passage that way."

I have more than my fair share of mother's stubbornness and Doser is my robot now, he obeys me (more or less) and together we convince Zamora to make the attempt. My spirits are high as we cross through the Fen and meet up with the trail to where the rivers flow together. I will do this my way and I'm even more pleased that I won't have to do it on my own. I solved my own problems, here and now, and didn't need mother to do it for me.

I avoid looking at the island between the rivers where Otu died and stare instead at the awesome sight ahead of us, the waters rushing headlong into each other, two rivers wrestling for supremacy as they course towards the sheer cliffs bordering them, channeling them so tight they flow swifter than the river that took mother's life. I gulp, thinking that maybe Zamora was a little bit right.

"Here we go," I say, with my brightest grin and starting forward.

"As you say, sister." Zamora follows me, her spirits not quite as lifted as mine.

The thing about distance in the real world is that it is always farther between two locations than your eyes make you think, and by early morning we reach the edge of where the shoreline fades away and rises into a sheer, perfectly vertical, rock-face. The thick stone is piled high, as if at a time in the long past this river was more powerful than it is now. There's a scattering of vegetation at the lowest elevation but then the slope becomes too steep.

Zamora's gracious enough not to say, "I told you so." Though she does cluck her tongue a few times as we study the scene. I'm about to turn away and admit defeat when I notice trampled vegetation on the opposite bank.

"What's that?" I point so she and Doser see what I'm seeing.

"It might be a trail," Zamora allows and we wait while Doser darts across the waters. He scouts for several minutes before returning.

"There's a ledge carved through the stone, from when the river was higher. It narrows considerably, but it does continue. I believe it may have been the giant's means into the valley. But it is not for us."

And he's right. I know. We can hardly swim to it. I bite my lip and avoid looking at either of them as I whisper, "Now we backtrack?"

"No. We would lose hours. But if we cut through the forest, here, we'll meet up with the trail. Kono may not catch us."

Kono.

My heart flops. I hadn't thought much about that but I realize I should have. Once he thinks we are fleeing, he'll come after us, and we have already wasted much time. My spirits sink, pooling around my ankles.

We ascend the other way, the original, way, and I see how right Zamora was. Occasionally we glimpse the river below; the cliff tall and daunting and the rock ledge rain-slick. A slip would send a gal tumbling into the waters.

We have wasted time. I've wasted time; I've jeopardized our escape.

Zamora stops us as we near the scout's watch post and we shelter beneath three stunted pine trees. Ahead, the rock wall climbs on, passing a large lean-to built from several thick trunks set sideways. Other logs have been piled up the sides, forming crude walls, though the front facing the trail, is open. The watch post is on the highest point of the trail, giving the scouts a view into the village valley and of the trail leading into the valley. Across the trail from the lean-to is a sheer drop off, spilling all the way down to the river we failed to cross.

Periodically a scout emerges from the lean-to, looks around, and then steps back, taking shelter from the rain. I recognize all of them, including One Eye, whose true name is Ricck.

Four young men between us and freedom.

CHAPTER 24

Easy Kill

The only obstacle stopping me now from returning home is these four young men.

(Well, okay, let us be honest... once past them we still have to brave forests teaming with monsters and then face the river that drowned my mother and then somehow cross a small sea, but those are concerns for later, right?)

Four deaths.

Simple enough for Doser to sneak up on them and use his claw to nudge one or two or three of them over. With the revolver I've pulled out of my sack I'm sure to finish any survivors if Doser is incapable of doing so.

This will be the price for my freedom.

"It must be done," Zamora whispers. I do not understand how she, who has lived with the clan longer than I, is so willing to commit murder. Perhaps a savage's soul is as calloused as a savage's hands.

I toy with the fringe of my sack, feeling the urn inside it. *What would you do, grandmother?* I have the feeling that she'd have rushed them, guns a blazing. That was her way.

It is not mine.

I'm sorry, grandmother, but not this.

"We can't," I say.

Doser's eye flashes red with annoyance but killing them is wrong and I know it.

"Then what would you have us do, Miranda?" Zamora asks. "We must not forget Kono."

Being reminded of the headman sets me to wringing my hands, as if by folding and unfolding my fingers I'll invoke a solution from the air. Had we planned this better I might have learned how often food or other supplies were brought to the men, might have pretended to be here for a legitimate reason and tricked the men, somehow.

I want to cry, I want to call home, I want to know that somebody is coming to rescue me. I don't want to be here, with lives, either ours or theirs, in the balance. Kill or be killed, like Otu facing down the giant and failing.

My hands still.

"Distract them instead," I say.

Doser blinks several times. "Simpler to shove them over."

"Simpler, yes, but simpler is seldom right, is it?" Yeah, I know, this sounds like something my mother would say; damned planet is breaking me.

I think the robot considers arguing the point but Zamora interrupts him.

"The path splits into several trails, on the lower end. Lead them north; Miranda and I, we'll take the main trail, towards the coast."

Bringing Zamora along was definitely one of my better ideas, though it hardly makes up for my failure earlier, the time wasted at the river. I was not thinking straight when the men brought me to the village and I have little memory of the trail at all.

Doser snorts and then darts out, plummeting over the cliff's edge. Zamora settles her hand on mine and I let her squeeze. I'm nervous too and I don't know what to expect. If the men see Doser will they chase him? Or will they send a runner back to alert the clan? Or will—

—a giant's shriek stops me from thinking about anything and Zamora grasps my hand tight, hurting me.

I almost panic.

But then I laugh.

"Miranda, we must be quiet," Zamora whispers, releasing my hand, staring at me as if I've grown a third eye.

"It is just Doser. This noise, he makes it."

"Are you sure?"

Of course I am. There is no way my luck is so terrible.

"Yes," I say, "he recorded it, earlier. Like our music, Zamora. This is Doser's distraction."

I don't know if she believes me but I urge
Zamora to rise and we creep towards the
deserted watch post. Here, on the trail's highest
point, we catch sight of the scouts entering the
forest, taking a northeasterly route.

"It is true," she whispers. Minutes later we
are running down the trail that will lead us
towards the sea. We avoid looking back,
reassured by the shouting we hear far off in the
woods, the scouts fooled into believing that
they track a giant.

Once again I'm running. Once again I'm
trying to avoid capture. There is no thunder or
lightning but the old terror is there inside me,
worsened now by a concern for the *thing*
growing inside me. That concern intensifies my
fear in a way I never might have imagined
possible.

One misplaced foot, one snared ankle, and
I'll tumble down the path, I'll injure this child
inside me. But if I slow they'll catch me.

Eventually we must stop.

I lean against a fir tree, my chest heaving and
even after several minutes my breathing does
not return to normal. Zamora sits, rubbing her
calves. There's no sign, none at all, of pursuit.
We are back in the forest and though I hate it, I
welcome the trees because they hide us.

We have to get moving and I gesture to
Zamora to stand but as I do I vomit, a thin
stream of warm bile splattering the grass. While

I recover, she rubs my back.

"Humans disgust me."

I glance up to see Doser emerging from the trees but that's a mistake because a spike of pain shoots through my head and I puke again.

"They've headed back to the watch post," he says.

I grin, despite the puke on my face. We are free of the clan! It is impossible but it is also true and I want to cry in delight except I won't, in case Doser's magic ears have missed a hidden pursuer.

"Once you are finished emptying your stomach, we should move on."

I puke three more times and then we resume our trek, no longer running but still setting a fair enough pace. Doser ranges ahead, on the watch for pursuers behind us or monsters ahead. There's enough light remaining, despite the lateness in the day and the clouds and drizzle, for us to find our way.

We decide to walk till we reach the sea and then from there head northeasterly till we arrive at the river. Zamora explains that after that she'll follow the river north to her clan's summer camp. She hopes to meet up with them before they set off for their wintering camp along the eastern sea coast.

"You should come with me," Zamora says but I shake my head. Partly because talking about this is silly when we haven't reached our destination and partly because I don't want to be swayed from my plan. I have trusted too many other people and now I must trust myself, despite my earlier failures. Still, I don't want to be on my own. I've always hated it and though I'm struggling to forgive Zamora for betraying my trust, I'd give (almost) anything not to be parted from her. But she won't dare come to the Tower.

And the Tower is, and always has been, the key.

We approach the coast but keep to the highlands that parallel the shoreline. With twilight settling over the coastal forest the Tower is distinct and visible, jutting unnaturally from the tumbling, alabaster rock of the island. It is a mark of civilization to me, a totem of the godlings's power to Zamora. She refuses to linger her gaze long upon it.

Eventually the sun sets and with night upon us, we begin our search for a suitable camp, finally settling upon a cluster of fir trees. Beneath their shelter we are practically invisible.

We light no fire and eat our hastily packed food cold; neither of us has much of an appetite. I gaze upon what civilized people call the Moonbay and I remember my dead family. I think we are near the crash site, near where Kal was slaughtered; I pray the forest is thick enough we won't have to see those places. Or Adira's pyre. This area is too full of painful memories.

I sleep but it seems the moment I close my

270

eyes I am woken by a hard shove from Zamora. It is still dark.

"Your golem has found a fire," she says. It takes me a mental moment to work out that golem means Doser and then I'm following the arc of her arm, as she points towards the north.

I rub the sleep from my eyes and stare until I see it. *There.* Higher up on the tree covered ridge leading down from the mountains is obviously a fire.

Several days later we have still not lost our pursuers. The scouts behind us set a hard pace.

I wake early to a chill morning and despite my fear and weariness I'm hard pressed not to be engrossed by the view as I squat, my back to the forest and our camp, peeing. The Orphan is full and her light blemishes the bay.

The tide is out, the water pulled away from the shore and in the blue-white light of the moon it appears as if teeth are emerging from the water, as if a fantastic monster is rising from the bay. The teeth seem polished, their tops smoothed into domes. I'm not sure how large they are but I think they might be sufficient to climb onto. They must be buried just beneath the surface when the tide is in, revealed only during low tide.

Adira would've known how they were formed. Would've known if they were a blend of hard and soft stone, perhaps once an undersea ridge. Thinking of my sister brings

271

tears to my eyes. This is another thing she would have loved to see, to experience. She always believed the Moonbay hid more secrets.

Finished, I set the revolver down and rise, tugging my trousers up, still staring at the stones as I do so.

My feet are right on the edge of the ridge, a hand on a leaf stripped birch, the other holding the revolver at my side. I've set my pack down beside me. Below is a series of rolling hills, maybe a drop of three or four meters, a gradual incline that tumbles down to the shore. We've followed the coast enough that we are now heading east again, towards the river.

My eye catches a flash of color below and I pause. Two beads of yellow are hovering down there, halfway between the beach and my ridge. A giant has been watching me pee.

"Hey, guys," I whisper but if they hear me they don't say and I'm afraid to raise my voice. I squat again and fumble for the revolver.

The giant takes several long strides, the driftwood cover growing sparser the farther he moves from the beach. The beast has massive shoulders and thickly muscled arms and three curling branches of horn rise from its head and down its back like hair knotted by, and full of, wicked barbs. The dead giant I saw earlier is nothing compared with this vibrant and dynamic creature moving towards me. I was right and Zamora wrong: it is beyond mere animal.

Its fleshy, bullet-shaped head, snaps side to

side, wide-nostrils testing the air. I'm glued to where I squat, not willing to take my eyes from it.

"*Guys*!" No point in whispering now, it is clear the thing is approaching me.

There's a snap of branches behind me but still no words. My fingers curl over the revolver and I rise, though my knees are shaking and if I hadn't just taken a piss I would've wet myself. Fear and excitement wage war inside me as I raise my revolver. This naked, ugly, beast will tear me apart, unless I use this weapon, forged from minds vastly superior to the savages and giants of Terrasta, a weapon capable of tossing out a stream of bullets, assisted by an artificial intelligence targeting system. On Terrasta the targets don't have equally intelligent shields to deflect the bullets.

An easy kill.

I have to do this and it is not mere concern for myself that takes command of my trigger finger. A primal instinct, a concern for the life inside me, the life I don't want, the life I don't care about, makes me squeeze the trigger.

Nothing happens.

I pump the trigger. Twice, three times, four.

Still nothing. I don't dare look away even though now I see the stream of saliva leaking out the corners of the giant's mouth, a great, frothing river of anticipation.

Flipping the revolver sideways, remembering every action movie ever watched, I force my gaze from the creature's swollen, yellow eyes, and check the safety, hoping I have not made such a foolish mistake. I have not.

My weapon should fire, my smart bullets should slam into the creature and save us all. But it is not to be.

CHAPTER 25

The Standing Stones

There's a whooping noise as a stone flies past my head and strikes the giant across the cheek. The large beast pauses, wrinkling its face into a mess, sausage-like fingers probing where the stone struck. It takes a step only to be hit by another stone; this time the throw is accompanied by a harsh shriek.

Zamora!

The giant flinches, steps back, knocking its head side to side, as Zamora continues screaming at it. She might be frightened too but she's not rooted to the ground, like me. Not frozen with her fear. She's acting.

It starts towards us again, but it moves as if in pain and I do not think it is the stones. It is Zamora's screams. It doesn't like them. I join my voice to hers (and really it isn't that difficult for me to muster a panicked shriek).

The giant lunges, a tremendous leap that shakes the ground when it lands. Another leap and it will reach us.

"Doser, your—"

But my robot is wiser than I and he's already figured out the giant's weakness. Doser activates every obnoxious tweet, whistle, chime, and horn that he has stored in memory. Simultaneously. He also illuminates all his lights. The giant swipes its head side to side, as if to dislodge the noise. Then it looks up and my voice fails me, because I'm not expecting to see tears of pain and panic streaming down its cheeks.

Though it would only take a step or two for him to reach me, he turns away instead, and shambles towards the coast.

"It has no bullets."

I glance at Doser and he explains how to slide the revolver's cartridge free. The empty cartridge. The savages didn't know what the bullets were for and probably tossed them.

"You were brave, Zamora."

She shrugs. "We should move on. The giant might try to flank us. And the scouts are still on our trail."

Again I'm reminded that this would be all the more difficult without Zamora and that once we part, I'll be on my own in this horrid world. I accept her advice with a nod and let her lead us forward, with Doser trailing and watching for pursuit. Later, maybe an hour or so, the three of us begin climbing the ridge. The bay is on our right and the forest to our left.

"How did you know the noise would frighten it away?" I ask Zamora.

She glances over her shoulder, wiping a sheen of sweat from her brow. "Sometimes my father and brothers took me with them. When they hunted giants."

"Seriously?" On Terrasta women are mistreated more often than not but they are never set directly in harm's way (unless you count their husbands).

She grins. "Well, maybe they didn't always *take me*, not exactly. Sometimes I followed and sometimes Kal, he discovered me."

I smile too, thinking of the child-Zamora, brave enough to follow the hunters into the shadowy forest. An entirely different sort of upbringing than my own.

I glance at the sea. We're not quite parallel with the strip of water-covered stones I saw earlier; only their tips are visible. Even in daylight it is a strangely moving sight.

"Do you know much about giants, then?"

"Our magician taught us, as children, that they were beasts created because a hunter failed to honor the godlings. But Kal, he used to tell me other stories about them. He sometimes tracked the giants, just to follow, to observe them. He was always interested in his world."

She pauses and I think she doesn't want to continue, maybe can't. But then she wipes at her eyes and resumes.

"He never thought the giants evil in the way the magicians tell us. More curious than violent, always examining everything found. Curious and strong and fragile, frightened by every wayward gust and unusual noise. Like children."

"Children?" I know children can be disgusting and uncivilized but likening the giants to them is borderline ridiculous. "Children in the bodies of monsters?"

"Exactly."

I wonder at that but don't have too much time to ponder it because Doser floats up to us.

"Enough chitchat, ladies. There are hunters behind us."

"Have they seen us?" I ask but Doser doesn't answer. Zamora does instead.

"Won't matter. They'll have heard us. The screaming earlier, for certain."

Doser says, "They will try to cut us off."

Backtracking isn't an option for us: that would only lead us towards the giant. Zamora and Doser argue whether to proceed or to slip back into the woods. I have nothing to offer. I know nothing about surviving. I've always followed the lead set by others.

I watch the waters slosh against the shore. It is a calm day, with barely any drizzle and even a few splashes of sunlight. I stare at the tops of the stones, a duller white than the bay itself, a darker smudge.

It might be possible....

"We could swim to them."

Doser and Zamora stop talking and look at me instead.

"Those rocks, in the water," I say.

"The Standing Stones, they are Nidawi's spear tips. She left them, for the time when she returns to make war against the clans again. We can't touch them."

"We must."

"Only a magician—"

"Shut up," Doser says, "Miranda has a plan and it is sound. Swim and hide behind the stones. The savages won't think to look out to sea."

Zamora doesn't like the idea but she lets me take her hand and lead her across the beach. We do not have time to undress and hurry instead into the water with our clothes on, Doser ahead of us.

If this were an outing, with boys and everything, I'd have squealed at the shock of cold against my legs, to get their attention. Now I have to bite my lip to keep from doing so, involuntarily. The water is frigid, but my body (mercifully) grows numb to it, as the water rises past my waist. I soon have to lean forward and start swimming and Zamora joins me. She's a stronger swimmer than I.

I haven't done this in ages but nobody forgets how to swim, and our trio moves steadily towards the stones. Their tops are larger than I thought, rising about an arm's length above my head and as wide as I am tall. The stone is also not as smooth as it looked, the weather and water has worn handholds enough that Zamora and I haul ourselves up a bit, not entirely out of the water, but enough that we can climb to the back of the stone we share.

Doser lowers himself; hovering millimeters above the water.

"Now we wait," he says.

Even with the stones to more or less support us our interlude is tedious and exhausting. We fight to stop the water from pushing us against the rock and our skin soon grows wrinkled and soft, making us more vulnerable to the hard stone. Our exposed flesh is torn every time the waves shove us into the rock. Worse yet, the stones are covered with conglomerations of mussels and their shells are like tiny daggers, flaying the skin from us.

With little else to do while we wait to see if the scouts traverse the beach in search of us, I study the Standing Stones. They march an almost perfect line, from here at the mouth of the bay, to the island and the Tower. It is almost as if the engineers grandmother paid to build the Tower intentionally set that looming structure on the same path as the stones.

The distance is hard to judge but I think it might be a few dozen kilometers. An impossible swim but with the stones….

Zamora taps my shoulder and I look. The stones block our view directly ahead but we have decent sight lines to the rest of the beach. The scouts have reached the shore, from the northeast, trying to cut us off, like Doser suggested they would. That we were expecting.

What we were not expecting is that the scouts have brought others with them. Including Kono.

"How did he—"

Zamora silences me with a stare. Not time enough for the scouts to run to the village and alert him. He must have already been following us. *Oh shit*. He discovered us because I wasted time trying to find a way past the rivers.

I'm trembling now and it has nothing to do with the cold waters. The mere sight of Kono is my undoing. He's carrying a spear with two others slung over his shoulders; several hunters have accompanied him and they are armed as he.

Having no choice we hold on. We hear snippets of their conversation and it is clear they are confused and do not understand how we have disappeared on them. Kono pauses and I fear he sees us, because he stares at the Tower for far too long. Zamora stops breathing and I do too, as we wait, until he turns his back on us. It takes almost an hour for them to search the area, but gradually Kono and his men continue on.

We wait a while longer then swim to shore. Halfway there I'm confident my feet will touch bottom, but I'm wrong and my head slips under the water. My body doesn't even try to swim again, it gives up, shuts down as if I'm a robot with depleted batteries. I stare at the white rock, a solid sheet of it, as if the bay is a man-made swimming pool. The white is intense, almost blinding. Strange, I think, that this is all that remains of a moon. Adira would've—

A sharp tug on my hair drags me back and as my head breaks the surface I spit a mouthful of water out. Doser clasps me in his grasper and he's squeezing tighter than necessary. Zamora slides up beside me, though she's too tired to offer more than verbal encouragement.

"Keep swimming," she says. How to explain to her — and my asshole robot — that my arms don't want to? That my legs don't want to? But Doser won't let go and Zamora won't shut up and with feeble stroke followed by feeble stroke I reach the point where my feet touch bottom, for real this time. Doser releases my hair.

"Would be embarrassing if you drown now." He glides to the shore while Zamora and I help each other stagger from the water, our clothing drenched and hanging on us like heavy carpets. With our legs trembling from exhaustion we both want to collapse but Doser chides us with an obnoxious honk.

"Keep moving, ladies," he says.

"I hate that thing," Zamora mutters as I briefly glance back at the Standing Stones. Were I not so exhausted, I'd like to think I might have dared the crossing here, but as it is I'm barely able to drag one foot after another, accompanying Zamora east, towards the river that killed my mother.

Zamora and I talk often while Doser scouts

ahead. Our conversation propels us ever forward, as first a day and then another and then a third passes.

We've lost some of our gear. Our grains and other soft goods are ruined but the dried meat remains edible and mother's journal, like all solid tech is waterproof. And since nobody except me can open grandmother's urn, her ashes are fine too. Everything is just wet, which is not in the least unusual on Terrasta.

We've long passed the site of Kal's death; I hurried Zamora past that without explanation but I don't doubt she noticed the remnants of the campfire and the scattered goods that Kono's thugs did not steal. The only allowance I made was an unspoken whisper, an apology to my dead sister. The past is what is it and I have to focus on the future and the trail ahead.

I stumble. The path is more rock than trampled grass now and this is almost the billionth time I've slipped since we struck out in the morning.

"What I'd give for a proper, paved road," I say.

Zamora glances at me. "A what?"

"There are roads, back home, like animal trails but made of… rock, smooth and easy to travel from one place to another."

We have talked sparingly of Earth, just enough to make it seem strange and impossible to her.

Zamora shrugs. "Here all… roads are rocky."

I grin at her simplistic explanation. Every task that needs doing here is more difficult than on Earth, the chores of survival have not been automated, simplified. The roads are rocky but I suppose they are still roads with starting points and destinations; it is just the traveling itself that takes more doing.

Late afternoon, four or five days later, we reach the crossing.

I'm grateful that we haven't followed the river directly, as we did with mother. Grateful that I do not have to pass by where I lost her, but there's regret too, for Zamora's crossing is no more than a day's walk north of where mother died. If she had been more patient many terrible things might never have happened. I'd still be happy me, swimming in medicated bliss.

"There," Zamora says. The river narrows, a pronounced indent between the two banks. More trees, primarily conifers, with their brilliant green needles, grow near it than in other locations. But all that vegetation is incapable of muffling the river's bellow or hiding the bridge.

Three trees have been chopped down and placed across the thinnest section of river, each log twice as thick as my arm. They are roped together with leather.

"Come on," Zamora says, striding onto the bridge. The logs rattle as she hastens across though I note with some relief that at both ends they've been secured to the earth with thick wooden pegs.

"There's no time like the present," Doser advises. He floats effortlessly over the river while I take a cautious step onto the platform and am immediately dizzy. This river that I see flowing through the gaps between the logs is the river that swept mother away. The logs shift beneath my feet, each step shaking them and threatening to roll them out from under me.

I stop halfway across. I'm still tired from our flight, from the swim, and now my legs threaten to buckle, conspiring with my doubts, as if both want to catapult me into the waters, so that I might share my mother's grave.

"Look up, not down!" Zamora shouts and I think these words are divine wisdom. I obey and the dizziness recedes. I finish the crossing.

The moment I am across, Zamora points south, at the Tower.

"That is your way," she says, then points north, "and that is my way."

I nod, my eyes glistening, though I'm sure I still hate her. Or that I should still hate her.

"Come with me, Zamora. Surely you must be curious about my world?"

She shakes her head. "Your path is uncertain. Mine offers shelter and protection."

I turn my face south. A brave Miranda would have continued on, immediately, then and there, but I hesitate.

"You could come with me, Miranda, instead."

CHAPTER 26

Finding Home

"No, she cannot!"

We both turn, startled by Doser's outburst. The robot is as agitated as I have ever seen him. He's twitching in mid-air, as if encountering low altitude turbulence.

"I haven't said I would."

"You are wearing your thinking face, which tells me that you are considering it. Miranda, you have had *chances*, too many times, to do the right thing and you did not. You must think about the consequences. Of wrong decisions."

I ball my fingers into fists, hot and angry tears filling my eyes.

"I'm the one living with those *consequences*, robot."

The robot (wisely) says nothing but Zamora does. "She'll be safer with me; we'll be safer together."

"Then, savage, you must travel with us to the south," Doser says, "you must not take her north. Miranda does not belong on this world. She's not made for it."

I almost believe the robot's words, almost accept them, because haven't I whispered the same to myself, many times before? I think if I were still medicated it would be easier to accept them, but I'm not and I can't. Because I have done what my mother and my sisters did not. I have survived. And that's not nothing.

Yes, I want Salva to hold me. I want to forget all this and pretend it away. I want to be delightful Miranda again, going to parties and dances and just having fun.

"I want to go home," I say and as Doser honks in victory there's a flicker of sadness, or maybe, regret, crossing Zamora's face. But she's a hard woman, as all the women of Terrasta are, and it fades in an instant. How could it be otherwise, these poor wives who suffer at the hands of their men, the weather, and the ordeals of day to day living? Especially Zamora, who longs for a child....

I touch my belly. I think of Salva welcoming me, think of how swollen I'll be. How I'll have to explain why I never waited for him, never let him have that first encounter with me. How I let men take me again and again, as if I were....

I bite my lip, willing the thoughts away. None of this was my fault. None of this my doing. Except I had prompted the marriage between Otu and myself, *I* had put that in motion, which means I put this pregnancy into motion, too. I'm confused and caught between the doing and the not doing but a thought reigns supreme, lording over all the others.

Salva cannot know.

And there's really only way to hide the baby from him.

Shit.

The decision is so frustratingly simple I want to scream in despair. But I can't and I won't, not now. I explain it to Doser, though no robot will understand what it is like to carry a child that the man she loves shall never accept. No robot can understand how hard this decision is but Zamora does. She realizes what the robot does not. That I intend to leave my child. With her.

She clutches my hand and tells me her clan will bring me to the Tower after the winter passes, after the child arrives. Doser's less accepting.

"You stupid, silly, brat," he says. "Your mother and two sisters have been killed. We don't know what's happening back on Earth. There's more to this than just you."

"And what can I do, Doser? Alone and pregnant? What if the Tower *has* been taken by our enemies?"

"You should do what your mother would. All that she and your grandmother built might be on the brink of collapse and you think only of yourself."

His words are true but I deny them with a

vigorous shaking of the head.

"If you have no concern for your own family then be concerned for those that you would turn into surrogates for the child inside you," Doser continues his lecture and really, he's quite good at it, the lecturing. "Think of the plague that has struck them. The timing of it all. This should worry you!"

He's right. I haven't been thinking about any of that but what Doser doesn't understand is that the very act of surviving on Terrasta doesn't leave much time or energy for the pursuit of other interests. The robot might be inclined to sleuth out every mystery under the sun but I need to worry about such *silly* things as eating and shelter and not being torn to shreds by mutant giants.

"It needs to be this way. After the baby is—"

"There may be no after," Doser says and then he turns away. He's not following us north. He's flying south, towards the Tower and I'm stunned and if Zamora wasn't tugging on my hand I think I'd have finally followed him, for he's all that remains of Earth, here, on my mother's, my grandmother's, planet.

Sore feet and nausea conspire to make me forget Doser's abandonment. Zamora's route brings us into the foothills of a range of mountains perpendicular to those cradling Kono's clan, though we are many kilometers from where the ranges intersect. These mountains, Zamora tells me, run all the way to the eastern ocean. Her clan's winter camp is along the coast, at the end of the range. But we march towards their summer camp instead, in the hopes of catching them before they migrate.

We sleep every night without a fire and eat our meals cold. Zamora is more attentive than usual, buoyed by the promise of the child I haven't had yet. To be honest I hadn't actually thought this out before but Doser pushed me into a corner. And it is a plausible solution. Leaving the child to be raised by a woman who clearly has love enough to give.

I'm not ready to be a mother, not until I am Salva's wife. And why should he have to raise a savage's child because of my mother's mistakes? She brought me here, not Salva.

Earth is less than a year away and I can survive that long. A doser, not *my doser*, will inject me each and every morning and I'll return to the land of bliss and none of this will have ever happened. Zamora will be happy with my child. I will be happy with my Salva.

Zamora supplements our rations by picking berries and grains and by the time we reach the foothills, almost a week and a half later, I wake feeling better than I have in a long time and I take that as a sign that I've made the right decision. This morning, Zamora still sleeps and after taking care of my bladder I wander the clearing where we camped for the night and stumble across thick berry bushes like I remember finding with mother, a million years ago.

There are few blueberries left on the branches, most of them have fallen to the forest floor, unharvested. I pick a few, eating more than I keep, but startle, dropping them, when Zamora, who I have not heard wake, tsk-tsks me.

"These are safe, aren't they?" These are the same as those mother picked; I'm sure of it.

"A pregnant woman, should not eat too many."

I roll my eyes. Zamora has taken a renewed interest in my pregnancy and last night I learned that eating certain fish causes birthmarks and that black walnuts make children have big noses and several other things I neither need to know or believe.

"Don't tell me. Eating these berries will turn the baby blue." The problem with superstitions is that they inevitably lead you down the road to well and truly silly.

"No, Miranda. You eat too many of these and you'll have the shits." She shakes her head and walks away, as if I'm the savage and not she.

Later, we eat a quiet breakfast (with a reasonable amount of the blueberries I picked) and then we are on the march again, moving higher into the foothills, following a ridge of tall grass between thick conifer woodlands, never quite entering either forest but skirting both.

"We're not going all the way up, are we?" I

ask, about mid afternoon after we've stopped for a quick lunch. I'm feeling more confident that I've made the right decision. As long as her clan doesn't try to keep me, as Kono's did, I'll be fine. And I'll bargain with them, using the Tower. Who cares if I give the savages technology they should not have? My new worry is that this trek might never end.

"See there, between those two hills," Zamora says and I shake my head at first, not seeing what she points at, but finally I notice a diagonal line where the foremost hill cuts across the rear. "The village is there, higher into the mountains than Kono's, but not so high that we cannot breath."

"Well, that's good, I suppose."

Zamora smiles at my confusion and points to the mountains. "Thunderbirds nest on the highest peaks and if you climb too high, they attack, stealing your soulspirit."

Or, I think, the air simply becomes too thin to breath, but I don't burst her bubble or anything. Let her believe in her godlings and giant birds if that makes her happy. The air is definitely thinner and chilly, but not the kind of cold that makes you miserable. Instead it is fresh and invigorating.

Still, I'd rather have my warmth, and I long for the summer I missed, because on Terrasta, the temperatures never climb past the low twenties.

"I miss the beach." I talk about bathing suits and suntanning and surfboards as we walk.

Zamora shakes her head.

"The beach, is for hard work. We drag the tidal pools and gather shellfood. Our hunters corral the great migrating sturgeon. We spend our days chopping and skinning and drying our food for the winter. It is not a time for idleness."

"Your world is dull, Zamora."

"Hard work is never dull, Miranda," Zamora says as if that's a truth and not a motto the headmen and magicians plant in the minds of children, to indoctrinate them.

Another day of difficult hiking passes but with it, my nausea, so I'm not complaining. Maybe it is the exercise or the crisp mountain air. I don't know. But my hunger has grown such that when Zamora decides to stop early, to have a proper meal, I don't argue with her. We even light a fire (well, she does) and warm gruel. But Zamora has grander ambitions than that. She fills our birchbark pot with water from a nearby stream and sets this beside the fire on a makeshift tripod. Zamora then places several stones near the fire, empties her pack and takes it with her, this time gone almost an hour.

When she returns her pack is full.

She pulls out several handfuls of wild onions and sets me to cutting them, while she whittles away at long stalks of what appears to be a cousin to celery. We drop the vegetables into the water and she adds several stones from the fire. The warmth the stones have collected heats the water.

"We're having a proper stew," she explains as she places whole herb leafs in. Last of all she drags out two dead birds from her pack and I wince as she sets to work cutting the blue-feathered creatures apart.

(I imagine that if the birdwoman was here she'd have fallen over in shock. Zamora chops viciously at the poor things.)

"You do not know how long I've waited to do this," she says, "how I've hated that old woman's birds. 'Do not eat them,' those fools always said. 'They are sacred.' They don't know the truth about respecting godlings."

I respond with a shrug; I have no respect for godlings, of course, but nevertheless I am relieved not to see any orange feathers.

"How did you catch these?"

Zamora sticks out her tongue, I know the gesture of disrespect is not directed at me, for she's facing west. "I did not catch them. I hunted them. Kono's clan, doesn't teach the women anything of use. Kono's clan makes weak women. I've kept this the entire time and I haven't forgotten how to use it." She pulls out a thin strap of leather but I have no idea what it is. She tells me it is a sling and is capable of hurling rocks, but I lose interest when I smell the simmering stew. My mouth fills with saliva and anticipation.

When the stew is ready we eat our fill and even though the cold rains commence before the sun sets, even though the winds are chill and brisk, I know I travel the right path. Zamora says we will reach the village before nightfall, tomorrow.

Yes, I've made the right decision, choosing Zamora over Doser.

Our journey is almost at an end and I'm eager for that, for the finishing of all this. After Zamora falls asleep, I rest my arm against my belly, against the child I carry and I accept the stillness. I swallow the clean air and hold my breath while I stare out at the wilderness that no longer seems so wild to me.

Tomorrow. It is like the day I left Earth, walking in on the sleeping robots. They were just waiting. Until they were needed. They were the future, at rest. They were a promise.

That's what tomorrow is for me. A promise of—

I gasp, releasing my held breath. There's movement. Not nearby, not behind me. But from within. My arm curls tightly around myself, around my child, and I fall asleep, grinning

End Notes

About the Author

Thank you for reading this work and I hope you enjoyed it.

I am a graduate of the University of Alberta's computer science program. With that degree — and my writing background — I landed a job, and had a great career, as a game designer/creative director with the role-playing game developer BioWare (Baldur's Gate 2, Neverwinter Nights, Dragon Age: Origins). After ten years I retired from the games industry to focus on writing short stories and novels. Since retiring I have won the Writers of the Future Contest and now have over twenty published short stories. I also do game design consultation for various companies.

I regularly blog about writing and game design at blog.brentknowles.com. Please stop by and say hi.

Discover Other Work by Brent Knowles

Novels

The Pool: Tower, the second book in the Pool series will be available early 2015 along with several other exciting novels, including:

Feast Wars The legend of the Wanderer begins with this tale of virtual reality gone askew. With most of humanity trapped in VR, the beleaguered survivors must confront the dark angels from beyond the stars who have come to claim Earth as their own.

Latelander Within a deep space colony long forgotten by Earth a young politician and his estranged wife uncover a terrible mystery that may doom the colony.

Non-Fiction

www.amazon.com/Lazy-Designer-Game-Design-ebook/dp/B005KCM7DQ/
Start a Career in Game Design Practical advice on starting a career in the video game

industry and improving your design skills. The Lazy Designer series continues with four additional volumes describing how to perfect your design skills, build environments, create engaging gameplay, write character dialog, and plan non-linear stories. The final volume contains specific advice to creative directors. A print version is available here: http://www.amazon.com/Start-Career-Design-Designer-Volume/dp/0987687174/.

Story Collections

www.amazon.com/Mama-Other-Stories-Brent-Knowles-ebook/dp/B00NREOEHQ/
Mama and Other Robot Stories From the plight of artificial mothers charged with babysitting human children, to the journey of a sex toy that has grown self-aware, these six stories of unusual robots in unexpected situations will challenge your preconceptions.

CONNECT WITH ME

Twitter:
http://www.twitter.com/brent_knowles

Newsletter:
http://blog.brentknowles.com/brents-mailing-list/

Smashwords
:http://www.smashwords.com/profile/view/BrentKnowles

Amazon:
http://www.amazon.com/Brent-Knowles/e/B0035WW7OW

Facebook
http://www.facebook.com/#!/KnowlesBrent